# HOW TO BE
# JEWISH

## Other Books by David C. Gross

*1,001 Questions and Answers About Judaism*
*The Jewish People's Almanac*
*A Justice for All the People:* Louis D. Brandeis
*Pride of Our People*

*Pictorial History of the Jewish People*—Nathan Ausubel
    (Updated)
*One Hundred Children*—Lena Kuchler-Silberman (Edited
    and Translated)
*The Hunter*—Tuvia Friedman (Edited and Translated)
*Love Poems from the Hebrew* (Edited)
*Dictionary of the Jewish Religion*—Ben Isaacson (Edited)

# HOW TO BE JEWISH

David C. Gross

HIPPOCRENE BOOKS
*New York*

*Hippocrene paperback edition, 1991.*

ISBN 0-87052-069-5

For information, address:
HIPPOCRENE BOOKS, INC.
171 Madison Avenue
New York, NY 10016

*Library of Congress Cataloging-in-Publication Data*

Gross, David C., 1923 -
    How to be Jewish / David C. Gross
    199 p.
    Includes index.
    ISBN 0-87052-752-5 (hbk)
    ISBN 0-87052-069-5 (pbk)
    1. Judaism  I. Title
BM565.G69   1989
296-dc10               88-36505
                      CIP

Printed in the United States of America.

*For*

*Those Jews who know little or nothing about Judaism and the Jewish people, but have a desire, no matter how faint, to know the basics.*

*And those Gentiles who have a genuine interest in learning a smattering of knowledge about Jews and their ancient faith.*

*For the reader, Jew or Gentile, who may be curious as to why it is that the Jewish people, after nearly 4,000 years, despite centuries of persecution and massacre, is still here and still teaching the ethical precepts first promulgated in the Bible and is still, by and large, confident that people are and can be—in the words of Anne Frank—basically good.*

*A generation of Jews has arisen that knows not the Torah; that knows not how to distinguish between the Sabbath and the weekdays, between the sacred and the sensational.*

—*Abraham Joshua Heschel*

# CONTENTS

**PREFACE**
Page xv

**INTRODUCTION: WHY BE JEWISH**
Page xix

*Discovering anti-Semitism . . . Generation of lost Jews . . .
Converts outnumber intermarrieds and assimilated Jews?
No way! . . . Ethical behavior, that's what it's all about . . .
Jews proud but abysmally ignorant of heritage . . . Judaism:
built on deeds.*

Part One: **WHY?**

**1. BASIC TENETS OF JUDAISM**
Page 3

*Youngsters sometimes bring parents back to Jewish life . . .
One solution: lifetime of cover-up until the end . . . The*

*three-part basis of Judaism: faith in God, following Torah's teachings, concern for Jewish people . . . Entering and leaving the Jewish community.*

## 2. THE WORLDWIDE JEWISH COMMUNITY
Page 15

*If there had been no killings and forced conversions . . . Jews feel kinship for one another. . . . Twentieth century: vast dislocations in world Jewish community . . . Today's Jews of U.S. and West now differ from the Jews of the 1930s and 1940s.*

## 3. THE JEWISH STRUGGLE FOR A BETTER WORLD
Page 23

*Being Jewish can be a happy, fulfilling way of life . . . Judaism is never stagnant; religious problems always arise, rabbis struggle for suitable solutions . . . Jewish tradition holds that people are God's co-creators in improving the world.*

## 4. THE LIFE OF THE JEWISH FAMILY
Page 35

*Living as a Jewish family . . . Work week versus the Sabbath . . . Synagogue service is more than prayer time . . . Friday eve candles, Sabbath table ceremonies . . . A day of rest is like an oasis of plenty in a desert of harsh reality.*

## 5. THE FUTURE OF THE AMERICAN JEWISH COMMUNITY
### Page 45

*Divorce rate among Jews: half that of Gentiles . . . Why is Passover celebrated almost universally, compared with Yom Kippur, the holiest day of Jewish year? . . . Is Judaism narrow in its approach? . . . New fellowship movement: wave of the future?*

## 6. THE JEWISH AFFIRMATION OF LIFE
### Page 53

*Being Jewish means daily affirmation of life . . . To save a life, all rules are suspended (except for murder, adultery, idolatry) . . . Were early American settlers following biblical model? Is Thanksgiving really a version of Sukkot?*

## 7. JEWISH ETHICS
### Page 59

*Passing ethical values from generation to generation: no easy task . . . Thousand years ago, Maimonides advised his children how to conduct their lives, stressing wisdom, humility, sanctity . . . Rigid versus flexible Jewish viewpoint.*

## 8. PERSECUTION OF THE JEWS
### Page 69

*Why so much hatred against Jews? Some say because Jews prick conscience of people; others say Jews are hated for their virtues, not vices . . . Tolstoy said Jews were "pioneers of civilization and liberty" . . . Meeting Judaism halfway.*

## 9. JEWISH ILLITERACY
### Page 77

*"Jewish illiteracy" in America is widespread . . . Edward G. Robinson sings synagogue hymn . . . Nazi's son is now a bearded, orthodox rabbi in Israel . . . Jews take on traits of countries in which they have lived for centuries.*

## Part Two: HOW?

## 10. JUDAISM'S CONTRIBUTIONS TO THE ENGLISH LANGUAGE
### Page 89

*Words and concepts: Kiddush . . . Kaddish . . . Yahrzeit . . . Yizkor . . . Kosher/Kashrut . . . Tallit . . . Tefillin . . . Yarmulke/Kippah . . . Bentschen . . . Bris/Brit/ Circumcision . . . Challah . . . Chupah . . . Holy Ark . . . Eternal Light . . . Star of David . . . Machzor.*

## 11. SYNAGOGUE RITUALS
### Page 99

*Going to synagogue for a bar/bat mitzvah, for an Aufruf, for naming a newborn girl, for a special prayer for the sick, for a wedding ceremony . . . How to conduct oneself in synagogue . . . If you're called to the Torah.*

## 12. TAKING PART IN SYNAGOGUE RITUALS
### Page 109

*How to respond to greetings: on Sabbath or holidays . . .
After being called to the Torah . . . If you carry or raise or
bind the Torah . . . If you cannot read Hebrew, pray in
English . . . Reading the Bible and the commentator's
explanation.*

## 13. JEWISH IDENTITY
### Page 117

*Jews join synagogue (and Jewish organizations) in U.S. to
show their identification with Jewish community and to
bolster own sense of identity . . . Participating in a
circumcision ceremony and in a Pidyon Ha-Ben.*

## 14. DEATH, DIVORCE AND CULTS
### Page 127

*Going to a funeral: the chapel service, interment, visiting
the mourners during shiva period . . . Another sad
moment: a "get," the Jewish divorce . . . Rabbinical
counseling . . . Children who get caught up in cults or with
missionaries.*

## 15. HOLIDAYS OF THE JEWISH YEAR
### Page 135

*The Jewish year begins in the fall with High Holy Days . . .
Sukkot, Simhat Torah celebrations follow on heels of Yom*

*Kippur . . . Hanukkah, Tu B'Shvat (Jewish Arbor Day),
Purim, Passover, Israel Independence Day, Shavuot, Tisha
B'Av.*


## 16. JEWISH REGULATIONS AND
## PERSPECTIVES
### Page 149

*Keeping kosher . . . Are these regulations really important?
Are they dated? . . . What are the Jewish views on women's
lib, homosexuality, autopsies, abortion, animals, birth
control, hereafter, ecology, slander, nudism, reincarnation,
sex?*


## 17. JEWISH HISTORY
### Page 159

*Brief history of the Jewish people . . . Abraham, the first Jew
. . . Slavery in Egypt, the Exodus, Giving of the Torah . . .
When Judges ruled, time of kings, northern kingdom cut
off, the first Temple destroyed, return to Jerusalem . . . until
now.*


## 18. THE RELATIONSHIP BETWEEN THE
## LAND AND THE COMMUNITY
### Page 169

*Israel and the Jewish people . . . special relationship that
always existed between the Holy Land and the Jewish
community . . . "Dual loyalty" an empty phrase . . . Special*

*ambience for Jews in Israel . . . "Next Year in Jerusalem"*
*proclaimed twice yearly.*

## 19. A CLOSER LOOK AT JEWISH RITUALS
### Page 173

*The functions of rabbi, cantor, sexton, gabbai, Torah reader, Shofar sounder, teacher . . . Breastplate and "rimonim" on Torah . . . Kissing the Torah or a fallen prayer book. Build a sukkah, bake challah, learn Hebrew, enjoy being Jewish!*


## FREQUENTLY RECITED BLESSINGS
### Page 183


## SUGGESTED READING LIST FOR FURTHER STUDY
### Page 185


## GLOSSARY OF POPULAR YIDDISH AND HEBREW TERMS
### Page 187


## INDEX
### Page 196

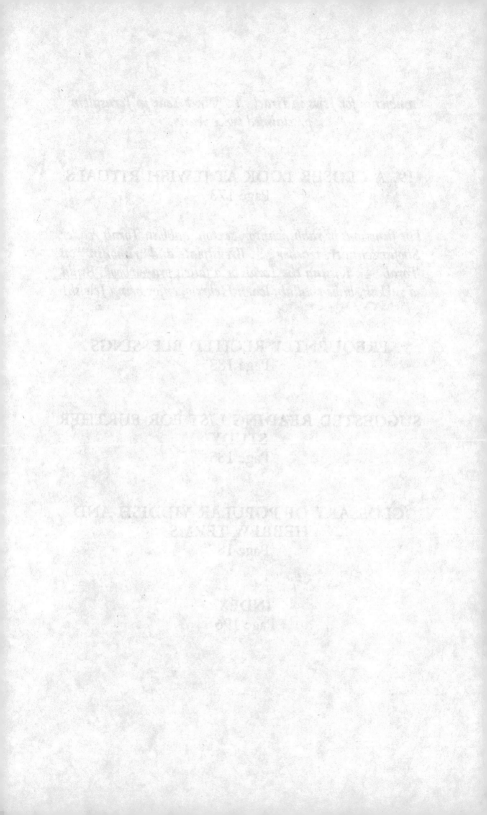

# PREFACE

THROUGH THE JEWISH PEOPLE'S LONG HISTORY, ONE strong motif has characterized Jewish teaching: Be an ethical, holy people, God commanded the ancient Hebrews. Fight hard against temptations of the flesh and against the fraudulent teachings of the spirit. Form a Jewish family; preserve and guard it; guide its members to a good, compassionate, moral life.

This fundamental premise of Judaism was first enunciated in the Bible, and was later refined and expanded in the Talmudic commentaries and interpretations. The thrust of the prayers that Jews recite, the goal of the rabbis' sermons and adult classes, indeed, the overall goal of Judaism and Jewish life—these have all remained constant. A personal and communal life based on the highest possible ethical conduct, characterized by compassion and justice is the bench mark for which Jews strive.

The world knows the Jewish people as the "People of the Book." It is true that there is a strong motivation among most Jews toward learning and education. The number of young American Jews attending college is much higher than the two-and-a-half percent of the total population that American Jews represent. The number of Jews who go on to graduate school continues to rise.

All this is good and admirable and a source of pride. Except that in America, and in the West in general (and certainly behind the Iron Curtain), a new phenomenon has surfaced in recent years. Jews may be educationally very advanced and at the same time can be culturally illiterate. Jews who earn their living as professors, physicians, lawyers, computer specialists, accountants, and so forth do not have the vaguest idea what Judaism is, nor have they even a basic knowledge of Jewish customs and practices.

Ironically, there are tens of thousands of American Jews, people ranging in age from twenty to eighty who do not know what a six- or seven-year-old student in a good Jewish school already has learned.

Over the years I have met many of these people, who are divided essentially into two groups: those who want to know at least something about their heritage, and those who really don't care.

This book then is for the former group, as well as for non-Jews who also may wish to learn some basics of Judaism and Jewish culture.

I wish to emphasize that I have written this in as easy a style as possible. There is no sermonizing, no preaching, no urging that anyone do anything as a result of my writing. I leave that to others.

My own intensive Jewish education ended formally when I was twenty-one and opted not to continue my studies toward the rabbinate. I chose the path of journalism and literature instead, and have written extensively on many aspects of Judaism and Jewish life in newspaper columns and articles, as well as in ten books that I either have written or edited.

I have continued for more than forty years to expand and deepen my understanding and knowledge of Judaism and the Jewish people, and hope to continue to do so in the years to come. When a new acquaintance, an educated Jewish accountant who held a top corporate position, asked me one day, in all seriousness, "What is the Torah?", I knew I had to sit down and write a primer for him and for the large number of people like him.

In the vast ocean of Jewish learning, I see this book as a first wetting of the toes. If you are inspired to plunge into a deeper, lifelong quest for Jewish learning and knowledge after you have read this small volume, I will feel that I have succeeded.

—D. C. G.

# INTRODUCTION: WHY BE JEWISH?

*Discovering anti-Semitism . . . Generation of lost Jews . . . Converts outnumber intermarrieds and assimilated Jews? No way! . . . Ethical behavior, that's what it's all about . . . Jews proud but abysmally ignorant of heritage . . . Judaism: built on deeds.*

WHY? WHY BE JEWISH? IS BEING JEWISH SOMETHING THAT will make you happier? more fulfilled? Will it lead to a deeper understanding of life? Will it guide you to a better relationship with your family, your friends, society as a whole?

Is it not true that being Jewish, in the past and probably now as well, can be a barrier to career advancement? Don't people in the public eye—politicians, actors, authors, and others—change their names so as not to sound "too Jewish?" Don't some young Jewish women have their "Jewish noses" trimmed so they do not appear too ostentatiously Jewish?

Of course, there are exceptions. Barbra Streisand, the lady

with the golden voice, displays her individual nose with pride. Noted author Irving Wallace, who was born Wallechinsky, must have had a deep laugh when his son, Adam, also an author, announced that he was changing his name back to Wallechinsky. Members of the Senate do not hide from the name Levin; presidents of major universities do not flee from the distinctively Jewish name Shapiro.

Yet many may ask, why be Jewish? Why perpetuate this ancient and admittedly remarkable religious-cultural heritage in the U. S., where it must remain a minority way of life? Why be different from 97.5 percent of the American people?

Why, indeed.

The answers vary: *So as not to give Hitler a posthumous victory.* After all, the Nazis systemically murdered six million Jews. The disappearance of millions more through intermarriage, apathy, and assimilaton will only make the Nazi campaign to rid the world of Jews and Judaism that much more successful.

*Be true to yourself.* You are the product of a unique family, the descendant of an ancient people that never has swerved from its original course: to bring a higher, ethical dimension to the world we live in. Through the centuries the contributions of the Jewish people to all mankind have been, and continue to be, disproportionately large. As a Jewish man or woman, you have nothing to be ashamed of. Quite the contrary, the Jewish people have been and hopefully still are an exemplary community. The Jewish way of life and the Jewish people are the roots of all Jews today, and they go deep into the past. Yet remarkably, Jewish teachings and insights are as relevant, as wise, and as provocative today as they were in the past.

*The nitty-gritty factor of anti-Semitism.* In the late 1980s most analysts of the Jewish condition in America agree that there is a potential for anti-Semitism in the U. S., both from the extreme left and the extreme right. Hence, one would think some Jews might opt to pass, to blend into the mass of

American life and pretend they are not Jews. Isn't that a prudent response?

Prudent or not, it doesn't work. Anti-Semites of all stripes always have been able to determine if someone is or isn't Jewish, no matter how strongly someone has tried to deny it. The Nazis proved that. Indeed, Jewish history contains many examples of Jews who found that the only way they could abandon their heritage and be fully, totally accepted by the non-Jewish world was by becoming either a notorious anti-Semite or an energetic missionary.

*The stubbornness factor.* The ancient Hebrews described in the Bible are said to have been a stiff-necked people. That stubborn trait seems to have remained intact with Jews today as well. *Davka,* just because, the world around us would like to see the Jews disappear, we respond by saying no. Why should we? We are nice people, decent people. Why should we disappear from the stage of history? Did we not give the Bible and its ethical teachings to mankind?

The world is big, and there has to be room for Jews to live as Jews. Zionism and the State of Israel, of course, are one huge answer to the problem of anti-Semitism and persecution. Jews in Israel feel free and unencumbered, and they are creating an exciting Jewish culture. If all the Jews of the world would move to Israel and live there as Jews, then theoretically there would not be a problem of anti-Semitism. Israeli Jews, born and reared there, do not think about their Jewish background. They are Jews because their fathers and grandfathers were Jews, as are most of the people around them.

But there are millions of Jews outside Israel, and the likelihood of their moving to Israel in the near future is slim. Most Jews in the world love and admire Israel and wish to see her prosper and be secure. But they also—by and large—want to retain their unique Jewish identity for themselves, for their children, for the future. There is an unspoken consensus among many Jews: We have made great contributions to

xxii      HOW TO BE JEWISH

society in the past, and if we are left alone, if we are not persecuted, if we can live our lives freely and openly and teach and study Judaism, we will continue to make great contributions.

There is also an unwritten code among many Jews: pride in the accomplishments of co-religionists that spills over onto all Jews. Sometimes this alone is enough to make some Jews active and committed members of the Jewish community, and turn away all thoughts of assimilation.

In a recent survey two-thirds of all Jews polled said they had encountered some anti-Semitism in the U. S. Some of those polled dismissed this phenomenon as of no importance; they had expected it, they confronted it, and then they went on to other things.

There are Jews in America today who react to anti-Semitism by fleeing from Judaism; there are others who have a diametrically opposite reaction.

The first time I ever came face to face with anti-Semitism was in Central Park in New York City when I was sixteen.

I had found a summer job selling ice cream and cold drinks in the park. The hours were long, from noon to midnight, six days a week. There was no salary, you worked on commission. In a good week when the temperature was in the nineties, sales were brisk, and you could earn as much as forty or fifty dollars a week—a great deal of money back then.

The day I chose to take off was Saturday, the Jewish Sabbath. I had explained to a fellow vendor that I was "religious" and that on Saturday I did not write or travel or handle money or do anything that could be classified as work.

We were perhaps some thirty vendors, ranging in age from sixteen to over fifty. The boss of the operation was a cynical man in his late forties who called me "rabbi" because I did not come to work on Saturdays.

There were a few Jews among the summer workers, and by and large we were a rather subdued lot. Many of us were the children of recent immigrants; our parents may well have been terrific people—but they spoke with a foreign accent, and subconsciously we must have been embarrassed. This also was a time when the Great Depression that had begun in 1929 was just beginning to wane. Jobs still were scarce, and we—Jews and non-Jews alike—were grateful that we had found work.

Overseas, an evil man named Hitler had risen in Europe and had shamelessly, brazenly branded all Jews as parasites, bloodsuckers, and God knows what else, and no one could be heard speaking up loudly and clearly to defend the Jews. In those days we were an introspective, cowed community. In the Midwest, a radio preacher with an audience of millions echoed Hitler's words against the Jews, and again virtually no one spoke up in their defense.

One Sunday night, after we had turned in our day's receipts, we were lined up to receive our week's commission. It was a hot, sultry night, and the boss apparently had been drinking. His face was flushed and his speech slurred. As each person moved up on line, he would fish out an appropriate envelope, push it across, and have us sign our names and step away.

When it was my turn he held onto my envelope.

"Hey, here's the rabbi," he announced in a loud voice. "Say something Jewish, rabbi," he called out. "I want to hear you say something Jewish," he repeated, his voice a drunken sneer.

I was embarrassed, ashamed, and at a complete loss. I stared at him not knowing what to say. From behind me a vendor spoke up. I turned around and recognized a fellow, whom I had come to admire. He was about eighteen or nineteen, polite, helpful, and had let it slip that his father was a police captain.

His voice was confident, calm, and strong. "Why don't you cut this crap out?" he shouted. "Give David his money, and let's move along. We don't want to stand here all night."

At that moment, he sounded to me like the voice of America, speaking up for justice and fair play.

My envelope was pushed toward me and the incident was

closed. Yet for the rest of the summer I felt different. I had been singled out because I was Jewish, or rather because I did not hide the fact that I was Jewish.

This book is meant for Jews, old and young, who do not have a basic knowledge of their heritage. These people find themselves in a synagogue or at a Jewish celebration such as a wedding or bar/bat mitzvah, and they feel uncomfortable because they do not know what the customs are or how one conducts oneself.

There are Jews who visit a mourner and have no idea how to behave, what to say, or how to try to console someone who has suffered a loss. There are Jews who are asked questions about their religion or culture or history or Israel by Gentile friends, and they are at a loss to respond.

Of course, there are Jews who come from homes where Jewish practices were nonexistent or utterly superficial, and who would genuinely like to learn more so that they could add at least a small Jewish dimension to their lives, and this book is for them as well.

This also is a book for Gentiles—for those who have an intelligent person's curiosity about Jews and Judaism—perhaps because of the relationship between Christianity and Judaism; or because someone close is contemplating marriage to a Jew; or because a particular Gentile reader is considering converting to the Jewish faith for personal, religious, or other reasons.

If some readers will pick up this book, glance at the title, and mutter to themselves that the author is full of gall, chances are they will be right. Partly, anyway.

After all, being Jewish is a relatively simple affair. The rules could not be plainer: All Jews—Orthodox, Conservative, Reform, Reconstructionist—agree that a person born to a Jewish mother is Jewish. Period. That's it.

Then there is another simple rule. Anyone who converts to Judaism also is a Jew, with the same privileges, obligations, and responsibilities as someone born a Jew. There are no differences in Judaism between someone born Jewish and a convert to Judaism.

Surprisingly, throughout Jewish history and stretching down to our own day, there have been quite a few converts who became leading Jewish scholars and pillars of the Jewish community. King David was the great grandson of Ruth, a Moabite woman who chose to become a Jew and live her life among the Jewish people. Nowadays, approximately ten thousand Americans opt to become Jewish every year. In most cases they become actively involved with a congregation or a Jewish welfare organization. Most of these converts to Judaism prefer to be called "Jews by choice."

Of course, on the other side of the coin, the number of Jews who are lost to Judaism every year outnumbers the converts. In the overwhelming majority of cases, the losses in the Jewish community are not due to conversion to Christianity or Islam or some other faith, but rather due to intermarriage and eventual assimilation into the majority culture.

The United States and the Western world as a whole reflect a society that is open, pluralistic, and accessible. Since Jews represent such a small numerical total in the Western countries, it is not surprising that intermarriage and assimilation are dominant factors in the shrinking of the Jewish community.

What is surprising is the tenacity with which so many Jews have held on to their faith and religious-cultural heritage. In many parts of the South and the West, there are synagogues and Jewish communities that date back to the early and middle nineteenth century where family memberships and traditions go back many generations.

But it also is true that some Jewish families simply have chosen the path of assimilation. Former Secretary of Defense Caspar Weinberger descended from such a family, as did Republican party leader Senator Barry Goldwater.

There is a contradictory, dichotomous situation going on

simultaneously in the American Jewish community today, and to a large extent it is being emulated in England, France, Israel, and some smaller Western countries. Like twin currents racing toward the sea, these dual developments are taking place almost side by side. One strong movement is the assimilationist-secularist phenomenon, usually manifested in young Jews marrying Christians and letting themselves gradually be brought under the influence of the majority culture. The other movement, weaker in terms of numbers but stronger ideologically, is a return-to-religion movement that usually is an adoption of an extremely Orthodox, rigid interpretation of Judaism.

In recent years the Reform wing of Judaism has ruled that if a person had a Jewish father and was reared as a Jew, he would be regarded as Jew. This ruling has not been accepted by the other wings of American Judaism.

It also should be pointed out that anyone planning to convert to Judaism and move to Israel should be aware of the fact that the rabbis in Israel recognize conversions performed *only* by Orthodox, "authorized" rabbis. Indeed, not all Orthodox rabbis in the U. S. will accept the conversions performed by Conservative, Reform, or Reconstructionist rabbis.

We return now to the title of this book, *How to Be Jewish*. Almost two thousand years ago, in the days of the Second Temple, the great rabbi and sage Hillel once was asked by a pagan to explain the entire Torah while he, the pagan, remained standing on one foot.

A cheerful, warm man, Hillel responded at once: "Do not do to your neighbor what is hateful to you. All the rest is commentary. And now—go and study!"

Essentially, Hillel's statement has not changed in all these years. Fine, one may say, but how different is this from what all religious or ethical movements teach? Don't they all preach ethical behavior between people? Don't they all espouse one version or another of the Ten Commandments?

In other words, if being Jewish—however one may interpret that—is more difficult than being Christian in America or Moslem in an Islamic country, then why bother? Why not just move into the fast lane with the majority of people?

Being a member of a minority group can't be as easy as being a member of the majority, especially if a person knows little or nothing about Judaism or the Jewish people.

Some sociologists insist that the American Jewish community is on the threshold of a new golden era when great cultural milestones will be reached, comparable to earlier periods in Jewish history. While it is true that the Jewish community in Babylon (now known as Iraq) produced the Babylonian Talmud during its exile in that country, and that there once was a flourishing Jewish community in Spain that had a golden age of literary creativity, the harsh truth is that both communities, for all intents and purposes, disappeared.

Although there was a Jewish presence in Iraq for many centuries, it was a community marked by oppression and second-class citizenship. Soon after the proclamation of the statehood of Israel in 1948, virtually every Jew in Iraq emigrated to Israel.

The story in Spain is even more poignant. In the same year that Columbus discovered the new world, the Jewish community of Spain, and later Portugal, was expelled. Many Spanish Jews fled to Holland, England, and the countries along the northern rim of the Mediterranean Sea. Eventually some of these expelled Jews made their way to the new world, settling first in Brazil and later in the colonies that would eventually become the United States.

Those seers who claim that a great golden age is on the horizon for the American Jewish community are wishful thinkers. Fifty years ago, major universities like Harvard and Yale openly discriminated against Jewish students, while today there are hundreds of colleges and universities where Jewish studies are taught. There also are Hillel centers and various Jewish clubs operating on college campuses. All this is true, but there is a very big but. Approximately one-half million Jews study at American universities, while the number who are enrolled in Judaica courses or Hillel or any other Jewish activity is minimal.

In other words, there are tens of thousands of young Jewish men (and some women) in the U. S. seriously and assiduously studying the great Jewish texts. But there are hundreds of thousands of American Jews, in their twenties and thirties and beyond, whose knowledge of what it means to be Jewish is virtually nonexistent.

Some of these people had a superficial religious schooling prior to a bar or bat mitzvah, while many others did not even celebrate this traditional rite of passage.

Sometimes one of these undereducated young American Jews finds himself in a synagogue. The occasion may be the bar mitzvah or wedding of a colleague, friend, or neighbor. Or it may be the solemn day of atonement—Yom Kippur— and the visitor in question is in the synagogue because he heard that on this holiest of holy days a special prayer is recited in memory of deceased parents.

Occasionally you meet some of these uninformed Jews at a Jewish wedding. Out of the corner of your eye, you notice how they try to understand what is going on. What is that curtainlike cover raised over the heads of the bride and groom? Why the cup of wine? What is the rabbi referring to when he talks about a *ketuba*? Why is the groom crushing a glass on the floor? What does it all mean?

There are lost Jews in America—people who have no desire to change their religious status, but who know so little about their communal roots. Strangely, many of these people are staunch, proud Jews who would throw a punch at anyone making an anti-Semitic remark. But their abysmal lack of Jewish knowledge is a great threat to them and to the Jewish community as a whole.

In recent years substantial numbers of young Jews have been lured into a wide range of cult organizations. The numbers are proportionately greater than the numbers represented by the American Jewish community. In study after study researchers have noted that the overwhelming majority of young cult recruits come from backgrounds where they know virtually nothing about their faith or their heritage. It is not hard to understand how a lonely young person, often away from home, could be enticed into joining a group that promised spiritual fulfillment and a sense of belonging to a caring community.

In 1938, when the Nazis marched into Austria to unite that country with Germany in the notorious *Anschluss,* the Jews of Vienna and other Austrian cities realized that they were in grave danger. The Jews who observed the holidays and the Sabbath, who attended services in the synagogue, who refrained from eating forbidden foods, and who sought constantly to learn about their faith, fought to survive. Some were arrested by the Gestapo and never were heard from again, but others resisted by seeking to emigrate, find a haven, and begin their lives anew. As practicing, knowledgeable Jews, they knew that such events as the Nazi *Anschluss* were not so unusual in Jewish history.

There were the other Jews, the nonpracticing, nonknowing ones, who were well on the road to total assimilation. When the Nazis entered the capital of Austria, the shock was too much for them. Many of these Jews chose suicide as a way out of the catastrophe.

The greatest challenge confronting the American Jewish community and Jews in other free, western countries is Jewish ignorance. It is far more dangerous than anti-Semitism.

A person can be Jewish without observing a single religious commandment; without ever setting foot in a synagogue; without knowing the basic teachings of Judaism, the history of the Jewish people, or the status of Jews in all parts of the world.

Truth to tell, some Jews think that by consuming large portions of Jewish-style food they are bolstering the Jewish community. Some who love the beat of a popular Yiddish melody, remembered from their early childhood, are convinced that this makes them good Jews.

Chances are that if you were to walk down the street in Tel Aviv or a heavily Jewish section of Brooklyn and ask passersby to define what it means to be Jewish, the answers will vary widely. One respondent is bound to say, "To be a *mentsh*—to be a real person, that's what being Jewish means."

Another passerby might answer that being Jewish means being merciful and caring about the welfare of other people. Still another, of course, would argue that being Jewish simply means following the religious rules of Judaism.

In a sense, all answers are correct. At the same time they all share a common characteristic: They omit one aspect that is really at the heart of the phenomenon of being Jewish. Very simply put, you can be born Jewish, you can become a Jew, but to be Jewish *you have to work at it.*

Judaism is a religion of deeds, of doing. There is no intermediary between God and a Jew. It is a one-on-one proposition. To be Jewish, in short, means to be as kind, compassionate, and ethical a person as you can be.

In order to attain that level in your personal, daily life, you must understand what Judaism and Jewishness are all about. You must learn the basics—the ABCs.

If after you have read this book you begin to realize how much more there is to know and to learn, then you will be well on the road to a healthy attitude toward your religious heritage.

There is a New York store chain that advertises "an educated consumer is our best customer."

An educated, knowledgeable Jew is the best guarantee for the future—for the individual himself, and for the Jewish community as a whole.

# Part One: WHY?

# 1. BASIC TENETS OF JUDAISM

*Youngsters sometimes bring parents back to Jewish life . . . One solution: lifetime of cover-up until the end . . . The three-part basis of Judaism: faith in God, following Torah's teachings, concern for Jewish people . . . Entering and leaving the Jewish community.*

DURING A PERSON'S LIFE, HIS OR HER INTEREST IN OR commitment to Judaism may grow or diminish. Many young parents whose children are enrolled in a religious school attached to a synagogue (a requisite in most cases for being enabled to celebrate a bar or bat mitzvah), have confessed that their "kids brought them back to Judaism."

An eight-year-old who can read elementary Hebrew, who knows the reasons for the major Jewish holidays, who has a glimmer of understanding of a religious service—such bright, motivated youngsters often have a positive influence on mothers and fathers who had gradually drifted away from active Jewish living.

There also are, of course, leaders of industry, often cut off from their early Jewish roots, who—generally later in life— wound their way back to a positive identification with the Jewish people. When a young St. Louis Jew named Gershon Schwab, the grandson of a rabbi, decided he wanted to study electrical engineering at MIT in Massachusetts early in this century, he knew that Jews were not being accepted. He applied under the name Gerard Swope, was accepted, gradu- ated with top honors, went on to become the head of General Electric, and for the major part of his life had absolutely no connection with Jews or Judaism. His wife and children were Gentile, and to the world so was he.

But he was a sensitive man and a thoughtful one. The reports of the calamity that overtook the Jewish people in Europe before and during the Second World War affected him deeply. The emergence of Israel a few years after the end of the war made a profound impression on him. Without fanfare he visited Israel in her early, formative years and decided that the bulk of his estate, valued at many millions, would be be- queathed to an Israel university of science and technology for the education of future generations.

To understand the situation of the Jewish people today, one need only look around and pose questions to friends, relatives, neighbors, and colleagues. There are Jews who enjoy being Jewish; those who love the rituals and the celebrations, the wisdom often heard in a rabbi's sermon, the insight gained in an adult education class offered in a synagogue or a Jewish community center.

There also are Jews who despise the fact that they are Jewish. Not many, happily, but enough to make heads turn. Often these are people who like to blame their shortcomings or failures on the fact that they were born Jewish. Judaism for them becomes an easy scapegoat. If only, they rationalize, they had been born White American Anglo-Saxon Protestants (or WASPs), then they really would rise to the top.

There are Jews in the arts and in the academic world who are proud of their heritage, and there also are well-known Jews who do everything they can to cover up the fact that they were born Jewish.

Of course, the Jewish community reacts to news of the day as a minority community generally does. When a Jew is awarded a Nobel Prize for helping to advance medicine or chemistry or physics, Jews as a whole take great pleasure in such an announcement; many are cognizant of the fact that the percentage of Jews who win Nobel Prizes is far above the minuscule percentage that Jews represent in the world.

But when a Jew is indicted or sentenced for a heinous crime, Jews feel a terrible sense of shame and revulsion. It does not matter that the individual in question was totally divorced from the Jewish people. The fact is that most Jews, even the most integrated ones whose roots go back many generations in America, are embarrassed when a Jew is apprehended and punished as a criminal. It often is seen as a negative reflection on all Jews. If the criminal is a practicing Jew, the community's shame and anger are especially great.

Well, then, a reader may ask, what is this Judaism all about that some love and others hate? What does it teach, what does it espouse?

Most people have a dim awareness that Judaism was the first monotheistic religion and that both Christianity and Islam are, in a sense, daughter religions of Judaism.

There is no doubt that most religions, Judaism included, share a similar set of values and precepts. In Judaism we have a religious faith—some even call it a civilization—that unites three basic concepts: God, the Torah (Bible), and the Jewish people.

In Judaism belief in God is essential. There are many names for God—Supreme Being, Supreme Intelligence (Einstein's phrase) among them—and many people have totally different ideas of what they mean when they use the word "God." It is a fact that there are secular Jews who say they love Judaism but do not believe in God. The Reconstructionist wing of Judaism, while quite traditional in its observance of rituals and customs, rejects the idea of a supernatural divine being. There are orthodox Jews, and certainly Reform and Conservative Jews, too, who obey the commandments, observe the religious rules, attend services—and yet, deep in their hearts, some and perhaps many are skeptical about the concept of a divine being. They enjoy being Jewish, they explain, and are willing to coast along for years, perhaps hoping that they will understand what the word "God" means later in life.

Without at least a modicum of belief in God, it almost is impossible to appreciate the Jewish heritage. The word "God" appears innumerable times in the Bible, in the commentaries and interpretations of the Talmudic rabbis, as well as in the prayerbook. An English essayist once wrote that God is the only character in the Bible. Someone else wrote that the Jewish people, for nearly four thousand years, have been in endless quest of God.

Belief in God is a personal, totally individual phenomenon. There were Jews who survived Nazi concentration camps, and when they came out they cursed God and rejected any belief in Him. Others, including some who had been non-believing Jews, emerged from Auschwitz professing a new understanding of God and opting for a religious way of life.

It probably is true that there are no atheists in foxholes. In the aftermath of the Yom Kippur War of 1973, when Egypt and Syria attacked Israel on the holiest day of the Jewish year, hundreds of Israeli soldiers who were unscathed in the fierce fighting resolved to change their lifestyles and became observant Jews. Nowadays one hears about people who survive a major illness or surgery and vow to attend religious services regularly and diligently. Is this a true belief in God, or is it an understandable human reaction to a traumatic experience?

The second of the three basic concepts of Judaism is the Torah. Strictly speaking, the word refers to the first third of the Jewish Bible, i.e., the Pentateuch or as it sometimes called the Five Books of Moses. But in its larger sense the word "Torah" refers to the entire Jewish Bible. More importantly, the premise behind the idea of the Torah is that these books or words, or "teaching" (the literal translation of Torah), represent God's instructions to the world on how people should conduct their affairs.

To put it another way, God created the world, and when He gave the Torah to the Jewish people at Mount Sinai in an episode that is usually called the Revelation, the Torah was seen as a guidebook to life. God did not merely create the world and then leave man to rule it as he saw fit. God gave him the Torah as a compass to show the way.

Most religious thinkers in Jewish tradition differ on what the Torah actually teaches and how it is to be interpreted and followed. The Revelation itself is acknowledged to be a turning point in human history and particularly in the history of the Jewish people.

The great Middle Ages commentator Nahmanides wrote, "Every glory and wonder, every deep mystery and all beautiful wisdom are hidden in the Torah, sealed up in her treasures." The founder of the Hassidic movement, the Baal Shem Tov, wrote that "the object of the whole Torah is that man should become a Torah himself." The Talmud states: "Turn it [the Torah] again and again, for everything is in it; contemplate it, grow gray and old over it, and swerve not from it, for there is no greater good."

The third and final precept that makes Judaism unique is the special role and place of the Jewish people. Judaism teaches that the Torah was given to the Jewish people but not exclusively for the Jewish people. The Bible is for everyone. When the Ten Commandments include the stipulation that "Thou shalt not commit murder," this is meant for everyone, Jew and non-Jew alike. Revelation at Sinai is interpreted as a moment when the Jews are chosen to communicate God's will to all mankind throughout all history. Because the Jews were given a special status, in Judaism's view, it is incumbent on Jews to observe extra, special laws that are not required of Gentiles. But the basic teachings of the Torah, for example with regard to ethics, neighborliness, actions between men and between man and God, apply to everyone uniformly.

Another key distinction between Judaism and other religious faiths is that Judaism does not begin and end when someone attends synagogue services. Being Jewish is a full-time, twenty-four-hour commitment. Practically every aspect of life is encompassed in Judaism's rules and regulations. As was said earlier, to be Jewish means you have to actively work at it.

What is apparent as soon as anyone begins to probe just a little is that Jews differ, sometimes sharply, in how they approach the three basic concepts of Judaism. There are those who feel closer to God than to any other aspect of Jewish life. Step into an Orthodox or Hassidic synagogue and watch how men, draped in their prayer shawls, seem to be praying with a fervor that almost is palpable. They stand at attention but their bodies sway as they whisper the ancient words of praise and devotion to God. They seem to be all alone with God, and sometimes they appear to have been elevated to a higher plane of being.

Then there are Jews who feel more comfortable with Torah, with the constant study of every word, every syllable in the Bible, with indepth probings for new meanings and understandings of what the ancient text is really saying to our generation.

What is fascinating and even incredible about the lifelong study of the Torah is the fact that although the words in the Bible never change, every time a serious student pores over a few lines or pages, new understanding generally follows, making the reading of the Torah an exciting intellectual pursuit.

At Sabbath services, a section of the Torah is read aloud

each week. By the end of the year, the entire Torah, i.e., the Five Books of Moses, has been read aloud to the congregation, and in most cases explained and commented on by a rabbi. When the year is over, the reading cycle begins all over again. Thus it is very possible that an observant Jew who attends services regularly will hear the Torah read aloud for fifty years. In other words, he will hear the same chapters, the same verses, fifty times. Amazingly, if the rabbi is commenting insightfully and explaining the text wisely, boredom will not set in. Every reading will be fresh and seemingly new and unique.

There are Jews who concentrate on the third aspect of Judaism—the people, the community, leaving it to others to deal with God and Torah. These presumably are the pragmatists, the realists, who are more concerned with providing food and shelter to the needy than to dissecting a spiritual issue. There are Jewish organizations that attract this type of individual, and benefit from their devotion and hard work.

The network of charitable, welfare, social, religious, cultural, and educational organizations that the Jewish community maintains is impressive. The Hebrew word for charity, *Tsedaka,* comes from the Hebrew word *Tsedek,* which means justice. In other words, charity, in Judaism's view, is simply a righting of a wrong, a bringing about of justice to replace injustice. If someone is seriously ill, in desperate financial need, or in grave danger because of anti-Semitism, providing aid will help to correct the wrong.

To be Jewish therefore means to be charitable, to give funds with an open hand to all those in need; and, perhaps equally important, to give of yourself to people who need support, friendship, encouragement, a light in a dark tunnel.

When Jewish immigrants first arrived in this country, fleeing pogroms in Russia and eastern Europe in the early part of the twentieth century, they were more often than not penniless. They worked long hours in terrible surroundings to provide a living for their families, and managed—despite their abject poverty—to put aside a few pennies every week, generally before the onset of the Sabbath, for those even needier than themselves.

Is it any wonder that the sons, grandsons, and great grandsons of these erstwhile, impoverished Jews continue their families' traditions and provide generously for numerous charities?

To be Jewish, therefore, turns out not to be an easy, simple decision. One must commit oneself to a moral way of life; one must decide to fill the mind with knowledge through study and the heart must be made glad through acts of loving kindness. To be Jewish also means that a person must plan to observe at least some of the rules and regulations that have evolved over a period of nearly four millenia.

Judaism teaches that one does not have to finish a particularly heroic or generous or charitable act, but at the least one must start. As a Hassidic rabbi put it, "Each person must discover his own way in Judaism and then live by its light and be true to the religion by being true to himself."

Throughout history, people who hated Jews said all kinds of insane things about them. Jews, they said, killed Christian children on the eve of Passover and used their blood for the Passover Seder ritual. Anyone who knows anything at all about the Jewish dietary laws knows that kosher cooks are instructed to wash away all traces of blood from slaughtered animals before they can be prepared for cooking and consumption. And anyone who has seen how Jewish parents generally treat their children, and other people's children, too, knows that Jews do not kill children.

This horrible blood libel against the Jewish people unfortunately has persisted through the centuries, and many Jews were massacred when frenzied mobs took to the streets and sought to avenge the "murdered" Christian children. Incredibly, in the early part of the twentieth century, in the small city of Messina in Upstate New New York, an attempt was made to revive this ugly calumny when a small Gentile child disappeared. Fortunately, the child was found safe and sound, and the small Jewish community in that city breathed a sigh of relief.

Another slanderous accusation often heard about Jews and Judaism is that the Jewish Bible reflects a religion that is hardhearted. An eye for an eye, some people claim, is a monstrous idea, and yet there it is, black on white, in the Bible, a typical Jewish ruling.

However, the fact is that, according to scholars and historians and specialists in the Bible, such a sentence never was carried out in all the annals of Jewish history. Yes, it is there as a warning, and hopefully it serves as a deterrent against brutality, but such a harsh measure simply was never implemented.

So if we brush aside the anti-Semites' wild charges about Judaism, the questions remain: What does Judaism really teach? What is the Jewish view on abortion or homosexuality or ecology or care for the aged or adoption or divorce or drugs?

In short, what does being Jewish really mean? What are the basic rules and regulations about marriage, ethical standards, religious study and religious service, and a wide range of subjects?

If Judaism has survived for nearly four millenia despite centuries of oppression against its practitioners, what does it offer its followers? Do Jews find in a Jewish way of life true contentment, inner joy, health, happiness, something of great value to pass on to the next generation? What about the difficulties of being Jewish in what is after all, a Gentile world? What about anti-Semitism? What if a son or daughter chooses to marry out of the faith? Does that mean the end of the Jewish line of a particular family?

One of the most memorable weddings I ever attended was that of a young Jewish man and his wife, a former Christian and a recent convert to Judaism. The young couple was very

much in love; their friends and relatives were happy to join
them in the ceremony and in the reception that followed.
Everyone, it seemed, was dancing, having a good time, wishing the young couple and the groom's parents well. But wait,
there was a flaw in this happy portrait: the family of the bride
looked sad, almost mournful.

From the bride's family's viewpoint, their daughter had of
her own free will abandoned the Roman Catholic Church, her
family's faith, to embrace Judaism. The bride's parents looked
torn apart. On the one hand, they were happy she was marrying a fine young man whom they knew she loved and who
would make her a good husband. On the other hand, she had
changed her religious affiliation and now would be Jewish.
For the moment, at least, the parents looked overwhelmed by
the Jewish-style wedding music, the Jewish wedding ceremony, the rabbi, the men with *yarmulkes* on their heads, and
the kosher food.

There are parents who react differently, to be sure; they are
perfectly happy to see their children marry whomsoever they
please. But it is safe to assume that a great many families, both
Jewish and Gentile, have deep-seated misgivings when their
children intermarry and give up the family's original faith.

Chances are that for Jews the pain is far greater than for
Christians only because the number of Jews who intermarry
and allow themselves to become part of the larger Gentile
community is far, far greater than the other way around. And
of course, our numbers are small and were reduced sharply in
the recent Holocaust.

Perhaps, then, this book will be of some help to those who
wish to know what it is that their sons/daughters join when
they convert to Judaism, and perhaps it will make some Jews
hesitate about leaving the Jewish community.

To put it another way, if a knowledgeable, practicing Jew
decides to give up his faith, that is his or her decision. I may—
as a Jew deeply concerned about the well-being and future and

continuity of the Jewish people—regret such a step, but, as they say, it is a free country.

What I find tragic and deeply disturbing is when a Jewish person chooses to leave the Jewish community out of ignorance. Certainly someone who does not know even a smattering of Jewish religious values, ethical teachings, history, philosophy, culture or what-have-you is more likely to turn away from Judaism. A principal goal of this volume is to offer at least a superficial knowledge of what it means to be Jewish, and how to be Jewish. Thereafter, it is up to each individual reader.

# 2. THE WORLDWIDE JEWISH COMMUNITY

*If there had been no killings and forced conversions ... Jews feel kinship for one another. ... Twentieth century: vast dislocations in world Jewish community ... Today's Jews of U. S. and West now differ from Jews of the 1930s and 1940s.*

THE JEWISH PEOPLE, FROM ABRAHAM TO TODAY, IS NEARLY four thousand years old. Why are there only fourteen million Jews in the world today? Look at the Chinese, also a very ancient people, and look at their numbers!

The explanation is simplicity itself: murders, massacres, forced conversions, voluntary assimilation. Some historians have estimated that had there been no pogroms, organized mass murders, burnings at the stake, holocausts, and conversions, the Jewish people today would number at least one hundred million.

The game of "What if" is intriguing. In 1938 a young Palestinian Jew left his home in Galilee and traveled to Vienna with two loaded pistols. His purpose was to assassinate Hitler, who was scheduled to lead a parade. The parade took place as planned, but Hitler was shielded from the thousands of cheering spectators—and the young, would-be assassin—behind the bulletproof glass of an armored car. What if Hitler had been shot and killed in 1938? Would the six million Jews who were killed by the Nazis in the early 1940s have lived? Would there have been among these martyred people future scientists and doctors, artists and philosophers, a discoverer of a cancer cure?

The facts stand out sharply and boldly. In 1939, on the eve of World War II, there were some eighteen million Jews in the world. When the war ended in 1945, there were twelve million; today, a half-century later, there are an estimated fourteen million.

Because the number of Jews in the world is so small, there exists a special kind of kinship among Jews. Certainly the diabolical goals ascribed to Jews in the obscene anti-Semitic publications like the Protocols of the Elders of Zion do not even deserve serious comment. There are no "international Jewish cabals" or plots or any other such nonsense. In recent years, whenever an anti-Semite would hurl charges against Jews, insisting that "the Jews own the banks" and "control Wall Street," you could almost hear a collective sigh from poor Jews that would translate as, "It should only be true!"

The president of Israel, Haim Herzog, likes to tell a story about himself. About fifteen years ago he was traveling in the Far East, representing a large Israeli corporation (he is a lawyer by profession). One evening, he was in the lobby of a hotel in Taipei, the capital of Taiwan, when he heard a slightly accented English announcement come over the public address system:

"Wanted! Wanted! In room 908, one for a minyan, one for a minyan."

Smiling, he took the elevator, proceeded to room 908, and became the tenth man in a minyan. A minyan refers to the number needed for a mourner to recite the *kaddish,* the special mourners' prayer that is said for a year in memory of a parent. There were nine other Jews in the room, he recalled, a few Americans, a few Austrialians, a few Israelis, and together they enabled one of their number to read the special prayer that requires a quorum of at least ten. International plot? No. A special feeling of kinship? Yes.

On a trip back to New York from Israel some years ago, our El Al airliner had to make an unscheduled stop at Reykjavik Airport in Iceland. We were permitted to disembark but not to leave the terminal building. It was late August, and I remember standing near the souvenir stand when I felt someone tapping my shoulder.

I turned to see a young American soldier, perhaps twenty or so. He was a private whose uniform looked too big on him. With his head he motioned to the large window that faced the tarmac. The El Al plane, its blue Star of David and Hebrew markings clearly visible, was surrounded by mechanics who seemed to be checking the giant engines.

"You just get off that plane?" the young soldier asked. His voice was very low, almost conspiratorial.

"Yes," I said, wondering why he asked, and starting to feel a little defensive. "Why?"

The soldier looked to the right and left, and when he was satisfied that no one could hear him, he said, "When is Yom Kippur this year?"

I smiled, and told him the date. He explained that he was the only Jewish soldier stationed at the U. S. base located at Reykjavik; he knew that the High Holy Days, which include Yom Kippur, usually fall in late September, and that the unexpected arrival of an El Al plane gave him the opportunity to find out when the hallowed Day of Atonement was scheduled to be observed that year.

The most turbulent period of Jewish history has been and continues to be the twentieth century. In 1904, when the overwhelming majority of Jews lived in Czarist Russia, Poland, the Baltic states, and the surrounding areas, there were terrible pogroms that propelled Jews to flee. Large numbers went westward to England, the United States, Canada, and later South America. Smaller numbers of ideologues headed for Palestine to reclaim the ancient Jewish homeland and lay the groundwork for an independent Jewish commonwealth.

In the ensuing decades the majority of the world's Jewish population has moved to the United States, where more than forty percent of the world's Jews live, and to Israel, now the second largest Jewish population center in the last years of the century. In the words of one historian, it has been a "momentous century." On one side of the coin has been the Holocaust, whose impact has not been fully measured, while on the other side there is Israel. Before 1948 the idea of an independent Jewish state was only a dream, one that very few really believed would become a reality in their lifetime.

American Jews of an older generation can still remember when ads in the help wanted sections stated quite plainly, "no Jews need apply." In the 1920s and 1930s there were resort hotels bearing signs that proclaimed, "no Jews or dogs." In the years before the onset of World War II, pro-Nazi sentiment in the United States, England, and France was sharp and loud.

The Jewish communities of the world in the 1990s will be different from those that existed prior to the Second World War. The savagery of the Holocaust; the largely indifferent attitude of most Western, civilized countries toward the doomed Jews; the continued existence of anti-Semitism both in the East and West—all these factors have hardened Jews' attitudes toward their neighbors.

It is said that the emergence of Israel in 1948 made Jews throughout the world stand taller and prouder. This historic phenomenon, the reestablishment of a Jewish state after nearly two thousand years of dispersion, has bolstered the determination of Jews to fight any and all efforts to curtail their political rights in any country in which they live.

Thus, there now are militant Jewish communities in the United States, England, and France who are watchful that no Jews should enjoy an iota less than full rights along with their respective countrymen. Only recently, to demonstrate how far things have come, a Jewish psychiatrist attached to the U. S. Air Force challenged a ruling that he not wear his *yarmulke* while on duty—an action that would have been unthinkable a few years ago.

Being Jewish nowadays is a phenomenon unique to the latter part of the twentieth century. Contradictions to the situation of the Jewish people abound. A sensitive person sometimes feels that there is a moving pendulum swinging back and forth over the Jewish people—and sometimes it brings good, happy news and at other times sad, even frightening tidings. Before you can decide which way to react, it swings again and the view is changed radically.

Paul Newman, the famous movie star, whose father was Jewish but who was raised as a Gentile, once was asked why he considers himself to be Jewish. With his famous blue eyes twinkling, he responded: "Because it's more interesting!"

It can be more interesting, but especially for those who know all too little about Judaism and the Jewish people, it can be terribly unsettling. Until not very long ago, there were people in the United States and in Europe—and they probably still exist—who believed that Jews had horns. When advised that such a belief was sheer foolishness, they would note that the famous sculpture of Moses, the work of Michelangelo, clearly depicts the great Jewish lawgiver with two horns jutting out of his head. "It's in the Bible!" these people insist.

The only trouble is that the biblical word *karnayim* has been mistranslated. The word means horns, yes, but it also means rays, and the biblical phrase refers to rays of light—and certainly not horns—that seemed to appear over Moses. How many Jews have been feared or hated or shunned through history because of this clear-cut mistranslation?

Contradictions abound. On the one hand, in the Soviet

Union, where an estimated two million Jews have survived seven decades of state-sponsored atheism and anti-religious bias, it is a miracle that Jews are ready to give up their homes and jobs for the privilege of being allowed to live freely as Jews either in Israel or in the West. In the West vast numbers of Jews, generally out of sheer ignorance, drift farther and farther away from their heritage.

The great hero of the Soviet Jewry movement, Natan Sharansky, who was imprisoned for years because of his demand that he be allowed to emigrate to Israel, learned Hebrew by talking through empy toilet pipes to inmates on the other side of a thick wall. At the same time tens of thousands of American Jewish men and women, college students in most cases, cannot even read the Hebrew alphabet.

The anomalies multiply. Years ago, before India achieved independence from British rule, tens of thousands of idealistic Jews backed nonviolent leader Mahatma Ghandi and rejoiced when India was given its freedom.

Before World War II when Ghandi was asked to speak out against the Nazis for detaining Jews in concentration camps, his answer was that the Jews should demonstrate their solidarity by committing mass suicide in the Nazi camps.

Like so many other people, the Indian leader neither knew nor understood Judaism. The Jewish religion is dedicated to life; it is a way of living that encourages a positive enthusiasm for living every day fully and enjoyably.

Even during the Nazi era, when Jews in the concentration camps and in the ghettos must have realized that virtually all hope for survival had vanished, they maintained schools, organized concerts, arranged for theatrical performances. Judaism always has been a strong affirmation of life. In Theresienstadt, the so-called model concentration camp that the Nazis set up for Red Cross scrutiny, there were a small number of young children. The rabbis and teachers continued to teach them the essence of the Torah and Judaism until the very end.

In Israel, where so many young people have been killed in so many wars, the language of the people says it all. When an Israeli is asked how's he doing, he often will respond, *marvichim chayim*, meaning, "we're making life, we're living, we're enjoying." And of course the famous toast that all Jews make when they pick up a glass of wine or something stronger could not be clearer: *L'chayim*, to life!

If it is true that one of the ethnic characteristics of the Jewish people is a particularly good sense of humor, and judging from the large number of Jewish comedians around this may well be true, then it must be added that this humor undoubtedly helped keep their spirits high during long centuries of persecution. Perhaps it all goes back to King Solomon, who taught (in Proverbs) that laughter is the best medicine.

# 3. THE JEWISH STRUGGLE FOR A BETTER WORLD

*Being Jewish can be a happy, fulfilling way of life . . . Judaism is never stagnant; religious problems always arise, rabbis struggle for suitable solutions . . . Jewish tradition holds that people are God's co-creators in improving the world.*

FOR A COMMITTED, OBSERVANT JEW, LIVING A JEWISH LIFE can be an extraordinarily happy, fulfilling experience. It also can be a very taxing and demanding way of life. Judaism lays down very specific laws and regulations about the food that may or may not be eaten, the clothes a person may wear, the prayers that are to be recited daily. There are clear-cut proscriptions on whom one can or cannot marry, how to spend the Sabbath, how to prepare and serve the daily meals, and what kind of dishes may be used. There even are rules about how to farm, how to harvest the crop, and how to allow the land to lie fallow every seven years.

In the twentieth century rabbis are kept busy responding to a wide gamut of questions that arise as a result of innovations in medicine, biotechnology, and other scientific disciplines. These responses—essentially rabbinical answers to laymen's religious questions—form a separate subsection of Jewish religious literature known as the Responsa. Thanks to the computer, it already is possible to punch in a question that in previous years might have taken months to locate an answer for (the Responsa covers thousands of rabbis and extends over a thousand years). Nowadays an answer can be found in minutes.

Rabbis today must struggle with new issues like artificial insemination (is it permissible? by a stranger?), gene splicing, organ transplantation, and many other issues that have arisen in recent years. In all cases, when making their responses, most rabbis seek to find a hint at the proper answer in a phrase or line or word that is in the Bible, or sometimes in a comment by a rabbi made generations earlier in a Talmudic commentary.

Thus, to be a good Jew means *inter alia,* remaining in close touch with all new, innovative, and modern developments in all areas of life.

Some Jews sometimes have expressed their embarrassment at what they perceive to be a weakness in the Jewish people: the lack of appreciation for art. Art, that is, with a capital A.

It is an interesting point, although recent archaeological finds in Israel have unearthed quite beautiful examples of artisanship: aesthetically designed household items that were crafted thousands of years ago and still are quite stirring today. The truth, however, is that Jews, by and large, did not produce great artists and sculptors, at least not until the nineteenth century, when Jews finally were given equal political rights with other citizens. Before that time Jews were confined to the ghettos of Europe and denied political rights.

The usual explanation for this artistic paucity is the inclusion in the Ten Commandments of the prohibition against depicting "graven images." Certainly this must have had an influence on some people. In early versions of the Passover Haggadah, where artists portrayed people seated at a Seder table, they went so far as to depict everyone with a bird's face rather than a human visage.

But I believe the explanation goes deeper. Judaism is not a closed chapter of a book nor a finished book, for that matter. It is a living, breathing, adapting organism. When a painter or sculptor finishes his work, he is finished. The piece of art he produced is done, and presumably he then turns to a new work.

Jews look upon the Torah and Judaism in general as an ever-changing, ever-challenging, ever-confronting way of life. Being a Jew is "never finished"; as soon as one problem is solved, another surfaces. Perfection, so to speak, is just over the horizon, and the self-appointed goal of a Jew is to keep looking for the idyllic. In the academic world, in literature, where change and commentary and interpretation are constant, as well as in scientific/medical research, it would seem that Jews feel more at home. There is a strong Jewish tradition that although God created the world, as described in Genesis, the world is far from finished and whole and perfect. The world's people, according to this tradition, are co-creators of God continually seeking to improve the world and make life better, freer, more fulfilling, and happier for all people.

Edmond Fleg, a French Jew who underwent a painful spiritual quest, wrote a lovely little book entitled *Why I Am a Jew*. In it he said:

I am a Jew because my faith demands no abdication of the mind. I am a Jew because my faith demands all the devotion of my heart. I am a Jew because wherever there is suffering, the Jew weeps. I am a Jew because wherever there is despair, the Jew hopes. I am a Jew because the message of our faith is the oldest and the newest. I am a Jew because the promise of our faith is a universal promise. I am a Jew because for a Jew the world is not completed; people must complete it. I am a Jew because for the Jew humanity is not fully created; people must complete it. I am a Jew because the faith of the people Israel places humanity above nations, above Judaism itself. I am a Jew because the faith of the people Israel places above humanity the image of the divine, the Oneness of God.

Fleg died in 1963. A long time before him, the psalmist put things differently.

> Who may dwell in God's sanctuary? How can we merit a place in His presence? Live with integrity, do what is right, and speak the truth without deceit. Have no slander upon your tongue, do not evil to others, and do not mistreat your neighbor. Spurn a contemptible person, but honor those who revere the Lord. Never retract a promise once made, though it may do you no harm. Lend no money at usurious interest; accept no bribe against the innocent. Make these deeds your own; then shall you stand firm forever. (Psalms, XV, 1–5).

Judaism teaches that the goal of Jewish education, the objective of all the rules and regulations and customs and ceremonies, is to transform the Jewish people into a "kingdom of priests"—a holy people, doing good, spreading good, setting an example for all.

This certainly is an exalted, difficult ideal to attain. No wonder there has arisen a well-known Yiddish phrase, which is usually uttered accompanied with a deep sigh: *Siz shver tsu zein a Yid*. Translation: "It's hard to be a Jew." It is true, it is hard. Living an authentic Jewish life, however, can be ennobling and very satisfying and can give a person the feeling that he or she is ascending to a spiritually and intellectually higher plane.

Over the centuries the Jewish tradition has been that man was created in the image of God and that man usually hovers somewhere between the animal kingdom below and the angels above. The principal purpose of Jewish life and observance is to propel us a little higher, toward the heavens.

There never has been a universally accepted definition of what the Jews are. Brandeis called the Jews a nationality; some have called the Jews a people, a race, a nation, a religion. In an article published in 1916, a writer said: "The Jews are a fact, they need no definition. It is the definitions of the others that are troubling. For them, you are one, inside and outside, a Jew."

In 1898 Mark Twain wrote:

If the statistics are right, the Jews constitute but one percent of the human race. It suggests a nebulous, dim puff of stardust lost in the blaze of the Milky Way. Properly the Jew ought hardly to be heard of; but he is heard of, has always been heard of. He has made a marvelous fight in this world, in all the ages; and he has done it with his hands tied behind him.

In 1934 Einstein wrote of the Jews: "The pursuit of knowledge for its own sake, an almost fanatical love of justice, and the desire for personal independence—these are the features of Jewish tradition which make me thank my stars that I belong to it."

In 1903 the president of the newly established Jewish Theological Seminary of America, Dr. Solomon Schechter, said of the Jews:

We did not invent the art of printing; we did not discover America, we did not inaugurate the French Revolution, we were not the first to utilize the power of steam or electricity. Our great claim to the gratitude of mankind is that we gave to the world the word of God, the Bible. We stormed heaven to snatch down this heavenly gift, as the Puritanic expression is; we threw ourselves into the breach and covered it with our bodies against every attack; we allowed ourselves to be slain by the hundreds and thousands rather than become unfaithful to it; and bore witness to its truth and watched over its purity in the face of a hostile world.

Eric Hoffer, the longshoreman-philosopher who once wrote that the fate of the Jewish people is an accurate barometer of where the world is headed, also said that the ghettoization of the Jews by the Christian communities of Europe actually ensured the survival of the Jewish people. It was only after the Enlightenment, when Jews were free to integrate with the community as a whole, that many Jews felt lost. They were ready to leave the stifling life of the enclosed Jewish hamlet behind them, but their Gentile neighbors were not quite ready to welcome them with open arms. It is providential, Hoffer wrote, that Zionism came along "in the Jew's darkest hour to enfold him in its corporate embrace and cure him of his individual isolation. Israel is indeed a rare refuge: it is home and family, synagogue and congregation, nation and revolutionary party all in one."

Thus, as the last decade of the twentieth century begins, we find the situation of the Jewish people filled with very mixed signals. While hundreds of thousands of Jews in the United States and other Western countries seem to lean back and allow the huge waves of intermarriage and assimilation to engulf them, scores of thousands of others actively fight to learn about their heritage and to live openly and proudly as practicing Jews.

The number of young Jews swept up into the cultic groups, and in most cases presumably lost to the Jewish community, is a source of deep shock and dismay to caring Jews. It isn't enough that the Nazis murdered six million Jews, now Hitler has a postwar, posthumous victory as thousands of Jews surrender their ancient faith to follow some hypnotic guru promising them nirvana.

But the picture is far from bleak. Walk through the theater district in New York, and there you see young men proudly wearing yarmulkes, buying tickets to the latest Broadway hit. You see the same young Jews, their small head coverings securely pinned, working as physicians in metropolitan hospitals or on college campuses, and as enthusiastic customers in kosher restaurants that seem to sprout up almost daily in places like New York, Los Angeles, Boston, Philadelphia, Miami, and Chicago.

A friend visiting his sister told of a unique experience. The sister lived in a suburb of New York, in Westchester County, and the visitor, who had been living in Israel for some twenty years, decided to attend Sabbath morning services in the local synagogue.

He joined the traditional service, was pleased to see how full the congregation was, but could not understand one strange "custom." Every few minutes, he explained, he would hear an odd sound, and one or another of the men in the congregation would rise, remove his prayer shawl, and disappear. Some of these men would reappear an hour or so later, while others never returned.

His sister explained the "custom": many of the congregants were physicians, and the sounds were beeper calls. They had been responding to emergency medical calls, well aware of the Jewish religious law that states unequivocally, "Saving a life supersedes the Sabbath."

Oddly, this particular congregation heavily populated by doctors is reminiscent of the system that prevailed heavily in the *shtetl*, the small Jewish hamlet of a century ago in eastern Europe. There were synagogues that came to be known as "tailors' synagogues" and "cobblers' synagogues." These generally were smaller, simpler houses of worship where people came, said their prayers, and went home to rest and were distinct from the larger, more scholar-oriented synagogues where the rabbi or a visiting preacher would deliver a sermon or a capsulized commentary on the Torah portion of the week. Presumably the tailors and cobblers of those days were too exhausted by their labors to be interested in hearing a gifted speaker.

In the very Orthodox section of Brooklyn known as Boro Park, where scores of thousands of Hassidic Jews live, there are hundreds of small congregations of many different types.

Quite a few Hassidic Jews have become computer programmers since it is possible to arrange one's own hours in this field; it would be interesting to know if there already is an informal "computer synagogue."

Are Jews especially alert to manifestations of anti-Semitism? Do they sense hostility even before it is articulated? Are Jews perhaps oversensitive to such negative, hidden expressions about Jews? The answer to all these questions has to be affirmative. Buried deep in the memory of the Jewish people is the obscene word "Holocaust." There is hardly an American Jew who does not know someone who has the Nazi tattoo number marking their Jewish identity branded on his or her forearm.

A recent survey taken among students in Israel asked whether they believed another Holocaust was possible in the future. Nearly one-quarter of those surveyed said yes, including all countries in their response. Another group, more than fifty-eight percent, said yes, but only in certain countries. Only twenty percent of the students said such a tragedy could not recur.

In all likelihood American Jews also are deeply aware of surveys taken in the United States in the last seven or eight decades. These polls determined the rise or decline of anti-Semitism in the U. S. Depressingly, the numbers really have not changed much over the years: One third of those surveyed consider themselves friendly and positive to Jews; another third quite openly is anti-Jewish; and the final third is "neutral," claiming to have no real feelings about Jews one way or another.

An Irish Catholic diplomat and scholar, Cruise Connor O'Brien, who wrote a splendid book on Israel entitled *The Siege*, spoke as plainly as he knew how. He wrote:

Anti-Semitism is an incurable Gentile disease—it manifests itself in rejection of the Jews. In the Middle Ages, it was church-inspired; nowadays, it's motivated by political considerations, and by a deeply rooted generation-to-generation negation of the Jews—not so much Judaism, as the Jews themselves.

In large parts of the world, Jews simply are *persona non grata*—let there be no mistake about that. Jews behind the Iron Curtain and the few still in Moslem lands are not free.

Perhaps that explains why there is often such a warm, hearty sense of joyousness at a Jewish wedding or bar/bat mitzvah reception. There is a pervasive feeling of being welcomed and wanted.

As an American Jewish tourist from a small Midwestern city said when he arrived in Israel for a first-time trip: "Suddenly, the psychological weights that I did not even know I was carrying on my shoulders slipped off. I felt freer. I was no longer a member of the Jewish minority back home—someone perhaps to be pointed to. I now was a member of the majority. It felt good."

In 1988 the Jewish population of Israel stood at 3.6 million. Because Israel is the only Jewish community in the world with a high birth rate, it is projected that the Jewish population of Israel in the year 2000 will stand at 4.5 million—and probably will equal or surpass that of the American Jewish community, where the birth rate is extremely low.

It is not a Jewish tradition to look into the crystal ball. "No one knows what the morrow will bring" is a firmly rooted Jewish concept. But one thing is very clear: the Jewish population outside of Israel is aging. The percentage of American Jews over sixty-five in 1970 was twelve percent; by 1980 it had passed fifteen percent. Chances are that by 1990 it will approach the twenty-percent mark.

It is entirely possible—regrettable, but possible—that the number of American Jews in another two or so generations will shrink and that the present American Jewish community, which numbered six million a generation ago, will gradually diminish to four million or less in a relatively short time.

Chances are that it will be a committed and observant Jewish community; what also is likely is that its influence vis-à-vis the nation as a whole will weaken. The figures make everything clear: a generation ago Jews were three percent of the population and we had some real political clout. Today, Jews represent about two-and-a-half percent of America, and although Jews are still influential, no one is quite sure how long this influence will last. As the general population grows, particularly among other minority groups in the U. S., the influence of the U. S. Jewish community is bound to decline.

One unique feature of the American Jewish community is its so-called "civil religion." Orthodox, traditional Jews observe the rules, regulations, and rituals, but according to one sociologist, most American Jews observe a peculiar mix of American Judaism that consists of the following components:
• A strong feeling of unity within the Jewish community and a sense of the Jewish people's uniqueness.
• A self-imposed collective responsibility for the security and welfare of all Jews.
• Recognition of the centrality of Israel as symbolizing the Jewish people's unity and sense of intercommunal responsibility.
• Regard for the enduring value of the Jewish tradition, however it is defined, and a commitment to its perpetuation.
• Recognition of the existence of internal and external threats to the survival of the Jewish people and heritage.
• The importance of *tsedakah*, defined as charity and social justice.
• A need to participate in the larger society, and the compatability of society with the ancient teachings of Judaism.
• Theological pluralism—the unimportance of ritual differences among Jews but the importance of an individual's conscience as a key to Jewish life.
Although large numbers of American Jews are affluent and therefore normally would be expected to support conservative

politics, in recent elections they seem to have continued to back liberal, progressive slates. There seems to be near-unanimity of support for a secure Israel; a very widespread feeling that anti-Semitism in the U. S. is still a serious issue; and the determination to retain the American Jewish community as a strong, viable, and vital force.

The specter of the Holocaust, together with neo-Nazi outbreaks in various places around the world and Arab terrorist threats against Israel remain ever in the background of the American Jew's mind.

# 4. THE LIFE OF THE JEWISH FAMILY

*Living as a Jewish family . . . Work week versus the Sabbath . . . Synagogue service is more than prayer time . . . Friday eve candles, Sabbath table ceremonies . . . A day of rest is like an oasis of plenty in a desert of harsh reality.*

THERE SEEMS TO BE A POPULAR MYTH AROUND THAT JEWISH husbands are the best there is—they don't beat their wives, they don't drink or cheat, they work hard and don't gamble away their earnings.

If only this really were so! To some extent, it probably is-- Alcoholics Anonymous, Gamblers Anonymous, and similar groups certainly have Jewish members, but chances are that proportionately there are fewer Jews than their numbers would indicate. Of course, a century ago or even a half-century ago, the idea of Jewish men getting drunk or becoming addicted to gambling almost was inconceivable. Certainly there were Jewish gangsters and even murderers, but they were the exception. Nowadays, however, as year follows year, and as Jews become less and less different from their Gentile friends and neighbors, the sad fact is that there are more and more Jews with serious drinking or gambling problems. There even are a small number of synagogues in the Greater New York area where local chapters of Alcoholics Anonymous meet, a sure sign that the Jewish component of the chapters is growing.

As the Yiddish phrase says, *Vee es krisselt zich, yiddelt zich,* roughly translated: "As the Christian world goes, so go the Jews, too."

Today, when drugs are so widely used, the challenge of maintaining a straight, Jewish, ethical way of life becomes more and more difficult. An affluent young Jewish family I know picked themselves up and moved to Israel after their fourteen-year-old daughter was found smoking marijuana. Horrified at their discovery, the parents had asked her where she had obtained it and she replied that her friend's mother gave it to her. The parents confronted the mother, a Jewish woman whose daughter was a close friend of the girl.

"Oh, don't get so uptight," the woman said to the distraught parents. "Everyone smokes pot. It's the in thing. Don't be so old-fashioned."

Within a few months the family moved to Jerusalem. The parents and their children, including the young woman with the forbidden marijuana, are now well-adjusted. They concede that Israel, too, has a drug problem but it is "nowhere as bad as it is in America."

This recalls a famous line by one of Israel's early heroes, the great national poet Chaim Nachman Bialik. In the early 1920s, when the idea of a Jewish state was still a dream, Bialik voiced the hope that in the future Jewish homeland there would be Jewish criminals and prostitutes and all kinds of other illegals. This, he said, would make the country "normal." Sadly, Bialik got his wish. Although the homicide rate in Israel is far lower than it is in the United States, there are enough other kinds of criminals to keep the prisons full. In that sense Israel has become very much a normal country.

That is why, in the frenetic pace of life that characterizes the final decade of the twentieth century, a truly Jewish family living a traditional Jewish life sometimes is viewed as an island of refuge in a turbulent ocean. The rhythm of the Jewish family's lifestyle seems to differ from the beat of the world around them.

No matter what kind of work the father-husband or mother-wife does the rest of the week, one day out of the seven days of the week becomes a family spiritual celebration. It begins on Friday, just before sundown, when the mother of the household kindles the Sabbath candles and thanks God for the commandment to light the special symbolic lights, with their aura of holiness.

Generally, her husband and children will be watching as she covers her eyes for a moment of prayer and reflection, intones the ancient blessing, and then, her eyes reflecting the light of the candles, wishes everyone a *Shabbat Shalom* or a *Gut Shabbes*. At this point her husband usually will rush off to synagogue services along with his son. If there is a daughter, chances are she will remain with her mother to keep her company and to help prepare for the evening's festive meal.

At services there is a difference in the ritual from the daily prayers. There is more joy in the singing, for on this Sabbath day—just as God rested on the seventh day when He created the world in six days—people, too, must rest physically, spiritually, emotionally, mentally, and psychologically. During the weekday services people are dressed in the same manner as where they go to work, but on the Sabbath people put on something fancier, something more suitable to a very special day.

The Sabbath eve service is not long. After the concluding hymn congregants greet one another with best wishes for a Good Sabbath and rush home. In many homes relatives and friends are guests on Friday evening, and sometimes strangers are invited because they are alone in the community.

In the traditional Orthodox home, and sometimes in Conservative families, too, the father will pronounce a special blessing over his children upon his return home. The male members of the family will wear a *yarmulke* or some other kind of head covering. At the table there are two loaves of *Challah* (the soft, braided Sabbath bread) and sacramental wine. Traditionally, the father (after first washing his hands) will recite the *kiddush* (an expanded blessing for the wine), take a sip, and hand the cup to his wife. In most cases nowadays, everyone at the table will taste some wine from his own goblet (although grape juice is acceptable for anyone with a restriction on alcoholic drinks). Then with a special, serrated, generally decorated Sabbath knife, he will recite the traditional blessing for the bread, cut into the *Challah,* taste a piece, and hand out small pieces to everyone.

Then the traditional meal begins. Not everyone eats the same dishes, but more often than not the table soon will be laden with gefilte fish, chicken soup, chicken, salad, side dishes, dessert, and tea or coffee. Needless to say, the meal is strictly kosher. Thus, since milk and meat/poultry dishes may not be eaten together, the coffee will be consumed black or else with an artificial nondairy creamer.

Between courses, primarily in Orthodox homes, the diners will sing special table songs known as *z'mirot*. These are songs of praise to God, many of which are in Aramaic, the ancient Semitic language that was spoken in the Holy Land some two thousand years ago. (Aramaic is close to Hebrew, but Hebrew usually was reserved for religious studies and prayers and not for mundane purposes. The best-known prayer that has come down to us in the original Aramaic is the *kaddish,* the mourner's prayer.)

For the Sabbath meal the best dishes and the best flatware have been put to use; the ordinary dishes and cutlery of the work week remain in their respective cabinets and drawers.

The table is covered with a good, usually white, tablecloth. The candles glisten, the diners are dressed in their finery, and together the family welcomes the Sabbath into their lives. It is not surprising that the Sabbath is called the Queen Sabbath. No matter how modest the home nor how meager the food on the table, there is a feeling around the table that all the participants are royalty and Queen Sabbath is among them.

People sit at the table and talk, eat, and sometimes sing. The meal never is hurried, and when it is over, everyone joins in the traditional *bentshen*, the after-meal prayer that is usually sung together, expressing gratitude for the sustenance just received.

In Orthodox homes, where electric lights are not touched on the Sabbath, there usually are timers that determine when the lights will go off and on. Thus, after the festive meal, the rest of Friday evening may be spent in conversation, or reading, or strolling if the weather is conducive. In non-Orthodox homes, depending on the degree of observance of a particular family, some people will turn on the phonograph or radio or television, and find that the relaxation that these modern devices bring are part and parcel of the Sabbath day's quest for rest and respite.

Of course, since kindling a fire is not permitted, smoking is totally refrained from on the Sabbath. On Saturday evening, as the Sabbath is being ushered out in the beautiful *havdalah* ceremony, after which it is permissible to strike a match, it often is comical to see elderly, bearded men scampering around for a cigarette after having done without for twenty-four hours.

On Saturday morning it is time to attend Sabbath services. These generally last three hours and include the reading of the weekly portion of the Torah plus a special Sabbath section (*haftorah*) and special prayers not recited at other times.

Festive occasions such as bar or bat mitzvahs, pre-wedding call-ups, and naming of newborn girls are celebrated at Sabbath morning services. A special prayer for the leaders of the country is offered, as is a special prayer for the welfare of Israel. Once a month an addition to the service greets the new Jewish month, voicing the hope that it will be a time of good health and happiness for all those assembled.

In most synagogues Sabbath services are a time for prayer, a time to gain a new insight into the week's biblical portion, a time to hear the rabbi's comments on the events of the day, a time to enjoy the singing of the cantor (in many Reform temples with the accompaniment of a choir), and a time for socializing with fellow congregants.

For many members of synagogues, membership means not only a support for a "house of prayer, house of study, and house of assembly"—the classic definition of a synagogue— but also a sense of belonging to an extended family. Congregational acquaintanceships often grow into deep, serious friendships.

Over the years regular congregants begin to see certain patterns in the synagogue. The thirteen-year-old boy who celebrated his bar mitzvah appears ten years later with a lovely young woman for his *aufruf,* telling one and all that they will wed in a few days. A few years later the same couple returns, carrying a little newborn girl who will be named in the synagogue. Such celebrations become happy events not only for the immediate family and friends involved but also for the whole congregation as well.

In times of joy fellow congregants rejoice. In times of sorrow they share in a member's troubles, helping to alleviate the pain and suffering.

For many Jews the work week rushes past in a frantic pace. Often the work hours are long, the pressures heavy, the rushing around breathless. Then suddenly it is the eve of Sabbath. Time seems to stand still, and the whole world seems to say: Stop, pause, rest, slow down, take this day of rest and imbibe it into your soul so that you will be better able to endure the pace and pressure of the week ahead.

Ahad Haam, the great thinker and philosopher, wrote that

"more than Israel kept the Sabbath, the Sabbath has kept Israel." The Talmudic rabbis taught that one should "devote part of the Sabbath to Torah and part to feasting." Some biblical commentators claim that the institution of the Sabbath—it is after all one of the Ten Commandments—was the first step on the road to abrogating slavery.

In the twelfth century the great Hebrew poet Yehuda Halevi wrote: "The Sabbath is the choicest fruit and flower of the week, the queen whose coming changes the humblest home into a palace." A memorable sight in Israel is the traditional scene on Friday afternoon as people hurry home from work, almost every person carrying newly purchased flowers to grace the Sabbath eve table.

The Sabbath afternoons, after the long service and the traditional lunch, are usually spent in walking or visiting fellow observant Jews with whom to while away a few hours before the day's concluding service and the departure of the Sabbath. Sometimes, depending on the time of year and on the weather, people will nap or read. Orthodox Jews do not use the phone on the Sabbath, so that the day becomes a respite from that modern tool of convenience also.

Among more traditional Jews, there also is the custom of the *Shalosh Seudot*. Late on Saturday afternoon, usually an hour or so before the end of the Sabbath day, Jews will gather in the synagogue for a light repast, a few songs, and to hear their rabbi deliver a brief comment on a subject of Jewish interest. During the summer months when the days are long, congregants will meet more regularly and often pursue a more formal course of study—either a Talmudic tome or excerpt from the Talmudic work known as "Ethics of the Fathers," a short anthology of ethical teachings.

For many Jews the departure of the Sabbath is a jolting moment. For some twenty-four hours they have been transported to a higher realm of life. They completely blocked out all worries about earning a living, all concerns about the state of the world or the state of their family or friends, and for at least that one day they escaped into a happy domain of song, prayer, study, good food and drink, and easy fellowship.

With the end of the Sabbath, the world, it seems, starts to rotate again, spinning its creatures in any and all directions. For certain people the world seemed to have stood still, at least for one day.

Of course, nothing ever is quite as idyllic as we hope. Sabbath-observing Jews whose sons or daughters attend public schools find themselves torn on the traditional day of rest. There is a big football game, the son announces. "Everyone is going," the young man says. "How can I stay home?"

Or the daughter, anxious to enroll in a particular college, learns she must travel there on Saturday, the only day that the college will screen new applicants.

There are some limited solutions to such problems. For some, the public schools become off limits, and their children are sent only to rigidly Orthodox schools. Some parents compromise: "You can go to the game in the afternoon, after you go to services with me in the morning."

Orthodox Jews tend to live in clusters near their synagogues so that they can walk there on Sabbaths and holidays. Conservative Jews in recent years are expressly permitted to drive to services (but nowhere else) on the Sabbath and holidays, so it is not unusual to see a Conservative synagogue's parking lot filled on Saturday morning. For Reform Jews there is no problem, since Jewish religious law (*Halachah*) is largely shelved, the main emphasis in Reform being on ethics.

There can be little doubt that to be a Jew requires extra effort, but it also can provide an extra measure of inner joy and serenity. This is not guaranteed, mind you, but dedicated, sincere Jewish study and observance of the rules and traditions can bring about an inner strength that cannot be purchased in the marketplace.

I remember my grandfather, who for all intents and purposes was not a man of wealth or success. He eked out a bare living as an itinerant teacher and raised a family of four sons and a daughter, all of them good people. He was a totally religious man, observing all the rules without question, his voice raised high in song on the Sabbath and holidays. He was happy with his lot, as Jews are taught to be. What he had all his life, at least in those few years that I knew him, was a sense of joy and a feeling of hope that were contagious.

Being a Jew in the full sense of the word—studying, performing good deeds, enjoying life, and sharing it with those around you—can bring in its wake a sense of achievement and contentment.

Perhaps the Jewish tradition about the Sabbath, which after all is a mainstay of being Jewish, has it right: "The Sabbath is the incomplete form of the world to come."

# 5. THE FUTURE OF THE AMERICAN JEWISH COMMUNITY

*Divorce rate among Jews: half that of Gentiles . . .*
*Why is Passover celebrated almost universally, com-*
*pared with Yom Kippur, the holiest day of Jewish*
*year? . . . Is Judaism narrow in its approach? . . . .*
*New fellowship movement: wave of the future?*

HOW DO YOU EXPLAIN THE FACT THAT THE DIVORCE RATE among Jews, although certainly high in comparison with what it was thirty or forty years ago, is still only half of that of the general American public? What does it mean that Yom Kippur—the most solemn day of the Jewish year, the Day of Atonement when each Jew feels himself being judged and decided over in the year ahead, a day of prayer and fasting—nowadays is observed only by an estimated fifty-to-sixty percent of the Jewish community?

Compare the Yom Kippur fast with Passover, the happy,

45

family-oriented holiday dedicated to freedom, when family
and friends gather around the festive seder table, recite the
Haggadah, sing together the familiar tunes, and consume a
meal characterized by special dishes symbolizing Judaism's
dedication to freedom. Passover, according to the best studies
available, is celebrated by an estimated eighty-to-ninety percent of the Jewish community.

As for Jewish philanthropy, the amounts of money raised
for a wide gamut of causes is staggering. Certainly American
Jews give to general causes like local schools, museums, programs to advance medical research, colleges, American Red
Cross, and the like. But when it comes to supporting social
welfare and educational programs for Jews in need—in Israel,
in certain countries overseas, and here at home—the totals
raised are vast. This is not to mention the funds that many
families spend when they join a synagogue. Membership dues,
tuition for the religious school, support for the temple's bazaar
or theater program or some such similar event, can easily add
up for a more-or-less typical suburban family to at least
$1,000 a year.

What is it about the Jews that is "different"? Didn't Shakespeare (in *The Merchant of Venice*) try to show that Jews, after
all, are just plain folks like everybody else? "Hath not a Jew
eyes?" Shakespeare wrote in the sixteenth century:

> Hath not a Jew hands, organs, dimensions, senses, affections,
> passions? Fed with the same food, hurt with the same weapons,
> subject to the same diseases, healed by the same means, warmed
> and cooled by the same winter and summer, as a Christian is? If
> you tickle us, do we not laugh? If you poison us, do we not die?
> and if you wrong us, shall we not revenge?

Are we different or the same as everyone else? Or are we
perhaps both at the same time?

Just consider some of the data. We are perhaps two-and-half
percent of the American population, so how come we have (in
1988) seven Jews in the U.S. Senate and twenty-eight Jews in

the House? How come there are more Jews studying in adult education courses attached to synagogues and Jewish centers than attending Sabbath services? How come an estimated two-thirds of American Jews have never visited Israel even once, and yet, in a recent survey, eighty percent of the Jews polled said that being Jewish was important to them because it connected them to all Jews? Sixty percent of those surveyed said they considered the Jewish people as an "an extension of my family."

Judaism is a religious faith of universalist values. A 1986 study asked Jews whether they agreed or disagreed with the statement "As Jews, we should be concerned about all people." The number of people who said they agreed totaled ninety-six percent. And yet, when Jews were asked to indicate how many of their three closest friends were Jews, fifty percent replied all three and twenty-five percent said two of the three.

Therefore, it would be fair to state that although Jews and Judaism are universalist in belief and theory, in practice they continue to be particularistic. On the one hand, ever since the Torah was given to the Jewish people at Sinai some 3,200 years ago, Judaism has sought to establish on earth a perfect world, a heavenly abode. Obviously the battle for this goal continues in every generation. There runs through Jewish tradition the concept of *tikkun olam,* improving or correcting the world. This is what we always must strive for, and in that sense Judaism sees mankind as co-creators with God in making the world a better and happier place for everyone.

So far, so good. But on the other hand, in the aftermath of the Holocaust of World War II, when fully one-third of the Jewish people of the world was destroyed by the Nazis while most of the world just looked the other way, Jews today possess a different kind of mentality. We are not exactly cynical, suspicious perhaps, but we see ourselves as survivors—even those who lived far from the war fronts and the extermination camps—in a world that has been drenched in Jewish blood for long centuries.

Perhaps the feeling that Jews the world over have that all of us survived the Holocaust explains why eighty-five percent said in a recent study that they feel close to other Jews, while three-fourths of the respondents added that they feel a "responsibility" to other Jews.

Yet when Jews were asked whether they agreed or disagreed with the statement, "I get just as upset by terrorist attacks upon non-Jews as I do when terrorists attack Jews," the number who said they agreed was an astounding eighty-nine percent.

Belonging to a synagogue or a Jewish organization is in essence identifying with the Jewish community, and even though at least half of the Jews in the United States do not formally belong to either a house of worship or an organization, the overwhelming majority of them feel themselves to be concerned, committed, caring Jews. As one might suspect, the degree of affiliation in the Jewish community rises with the smallness of a particular community. Jewish families living in a small city like Waterloo, Iowa, are more likely to be members of the local synagogue and local chapters of national Jewish groups than their co-religionists in New York, Los Angeles, or Chicago.

The story was reported some years ago of a young New York Jew, a college freshman who lived humbly in New York with his widowed father. The young man had been attending class for a few weeks when tragedy stuck. His remaining parent was killed in a hit-and-run accident. Suddenly, the eighteen-year-old boy was alone in the world; there were no close friends or relatives.

In Judaism, a son in such circumstances is required to recite the mourner's *kaddish* prayer every day for a period of eleven months. The young mourner began to recite the prayer in a local synagogue. He would arrive before seven in the morning, don his *tefillin* and *tallit,* and say the prayers surrounded by other mourners intoning the same words. In the evening he would return for the evening service.

After a few weeks, he dropped out of school. He felt restless, cast off, a solitary piece of driftwood in a vast ocean. He began to visit other area synagogues in other parts of the city, and slowly he began to expand his horizons. He closed up his apartment and started to travel throughout the United States, stopping in cities large and small where he could recite the requisite *kaddish* prayer for his father. As the weeks became months, he found himself traversing the entire Eastern Seaboard, and then veering westward across the southern states until he got to California, at which point he headed first north and then east, back to New York.

Wherever he went, he recounted later, he found a synagogue where he could pray and recite the mourner's prayer. In some congregations he was greeted warmly, and in some lukewarmly. When it became clear to people that he was who he said he was—a young, unattached Jew from New York who was traveling around the country, saying *kaddish* in scores of synagogues throughout the United States—he often was invited to breakfasts and dinners, and was made to feel welcome in one community after another.

He had the feeling, he explained later, that he was a member of a huge family. It was that sense of caring and concern that helped him through the difficult months of sudden, total orphanhood.

The Bible advises us (in Ecclesiastes) to "eat, drink, and be merry." The Talmud seeks to teach us that the world was created by ten things: Compassion, wisdom, understanding, reason, strength, rebuke, might, righteousness, judgment, and loving-kindness.

Although Jews gave the Bible—certainly the Jewish people's principal contribution to society—to the world, large numbers of Jews possess only a superficial knowledge of the Bible and its world of commentators and interpreters.

The American author-scholar Lewis Browne said of the Bible, "When read intelligently the Bible reveals itself as the immortal epic of a people's confused, faltering but indomitable struggle after a nobler life in a happier world."

A century ago, Heine wrote:

> I owe my enlightenment entirely to an old, simple book, as plain and modest as nature itself . . . a book as weekday-like and unpretending as the sun which warms us or the bread which nourishes us; a book which greets us with all the intimate confidence, blessed affection and kind glance of an old grandmother. . . . This is called with cause the Holy Scripture. He who lost his God may find Him again in this book, and he who has never known Him will inhale here the breath of God's word. The Jews who are connoisseurs of valuables knew very well what they were about when—in the conflagration of the Second Temple—they left the gold and silver vessels of sacrifice, the candelabra and lamps, even the High Priest's breastplate with its large jewels, and rescued only the Bible. This was the real treasure of the Temple.

Rabbi Aryeh Kaplan, a brilliant young scholar who died prematurely, was an outstanding student as a youngster, and great scholarly innovations were expected of him. When he reached his late teens, he made a complete turnaround in his focus of interests and lifestyle and devoted himself to secular studies, emerging in a relatively short time as one of America's leading nuclear physicists. He held a senior post in U.S. government research, and again his colleagues expected outstanding achievements from him. Again, quite suddenly, he reversed himself and returned to the world of Judaic study, giving up on nuclear physics. In the brief period of a decade, he produced numerous books, translations, and commentaries, of which perhaps the most notable is his new translation of the Torah, called appropriately *The Living Torah*.

"More than any other force," he wrote, "it has been the Torah that has molded the Jewish people. The Torah is not a dead ancient document but a living testimony to a vital tradition. If the Jews are the 'People of the Book' then their book is the Torah."

Ironically, a great part of the American Jewish community,

for all intents and purposes, ceases studying the Torah after their early teens, usually when they celebrate their bar or bat mitzvah. Unless they attend religious services regularly, and are fortunate enough to have a provocative, insightful rabbi who teaches and interprets the weekly biblical reading with élan, chances are that their memories of the Bible will remain on a very childish level.

Here and there are exceptions to the rule. For example, in New York City there are regular weekly Torah luncheon meetings, during which some businessmen and professional people meet for two hours, allowing fifteen minutes for a sandwich and coffee and the rest of the time devoted to a visiting rabbi-teacher who will elucidate a sentence or two from the Bible.

In recent years there has sprung up a new kind of group, the *Havurah,* best translated as a "fellowship," where the emphasis also is on mutual study and social support. There are such groups in all parts of the country. They include young and middle-aged Jews who feel a lack of knowledge of Judaism's sacred texts and who also often find their lives to be lonely, even though they may be surrounded by many people. The *Havurah* groups often organize prayer services that are less formal than traditional synagogue services, in addition to their programs of study and social contact.

In ancient times, when Jews lived in exile in Babylonia after the destruction of the First Temple in the year 586 B.C.E., it was customary for Jewish farmers to spend their nonproductive winter months in a special communal educational program—an early kind of retreat where men who labored with their hands all through the year would be afforded an opportunity to delve into Judaism's biblical treasures. The *Havurah* movement reflects the same kind of quest for knowledge.

There are historians who see in the establishment of the United States a modern-day version of Bible times. It is true that Hebrew was a required language of study at Harvard, Yale, and Columbia (called at first Kings), the first universities that sprang up. It also is true that the very first book printed in America was the *Bay Psalm Book,* which appeared in 1640.

Then there was a time when some of the early founding fathers discussed the feasibility of the national language of the new American republic being Hebrew.

Indeed, biblical place names now are found all over the United States. And rabbis have led the daily prayer openings of Congress and of various state legislative bodies together with their Christian colleagues.

There can be little doubt that Jews and Judaism have played important roles in the development of the United States and continue to do so. On the other hand, if we look back we may well come to the conclusion that as wonderful as the United States has been for the Jewish community—and there is no doubt that the American Jewish community is the biggest, strongest and most influential in nearly two millenia of exile and dispersion—what also is true is that there lurks a great danger of the community's being swallowed up by virtue of America's pluralism, freedom, and openness.

To be Jewish in America today means to set out to follow certain religious/cultural rules, regulations, and traditions, for the dual purpose of attaining a high ethical code of living and personal and family happiness as well as for the purpose of preserving the Jewish community as a community. In other words, yes, there are other ways of attaining a high ethical plane of living besides Judaism. There also are other ways of being happy—personally and with one's family—outside of Judaism. But if one feels that the Jewish people deserve to continue living individually and distinctly as a separate religious-cultural group, both because of what they have achieved in the past and what they still can do today and in the future—qua Jews—then the ideal of living as a Jew and being Jewish becomes a worthwhile and attainable goal. There is another strong motivation in the Jewish community: Jews stubbornly refuse to give the Nazis a posthumous victory. The decline and disappearance of the Jewish community, even benignly, would be such a victory.

# 6. THE JEWISH AFFIRMATION OF LIFE

*Being Jewish means daily affirmation of life . . . To save a life, all rules are suspended (except for murder, adultery, idolatry) . . . Were early American settlers following biblical model? Is Thanksgiving really a version of Sukkot?*

BEING JEWISH AND LIVING AS A JEW MEAN AFFIRMING LIFE every day. Judaism is a life-affirming way of life that stresses the solution of practical, worldly problems of life on earth.

For the Orthodox Jew, there are actually 613 *mitzvot* or commandments that need to be observed. However, a great majority of them deal with Temple rules and regulations, and since the Holy Temple no longer exists in Jerusalem, the number of rules that need to be followed drops to about two hundred.

What are some of these *mitzvot*, these ordinances? The first rule is to be fruitful and multiply. The second commandment deals with the need for a newborn male child, at eight days of age, to be circumcised. Rules follow about keeping the Sabbath; preparations for Passover; charity for the poor; marriage and divorce; affixing a mezuzah to the doorpost; being a holy people; abstaining from murder, adultery, stealing, false testimony, and covetousness.

The rules go on and on: do not place an obstacle before a blind man, do not curse the deaf, do not carry tales, do not lie, do not use God's name in vain, do not wear clothes of members of the opposite sex, do not work or eat or drink on the Day of Atonement.

The do's and don't's go on and on, and of course the number of people who observe each and every rule meticulously is undoubtedly small. Nonetheless, Jewish tradition says that we should do the best we can and as much as we can, and if we cannot follow all the rules this does not mean that we should abandon them all. On the contrary, one should do the minimum that one can in the belief that with the passage of time doing more will become easier and/or more desirable.

A Jew remains a Jew even if he does not observe any of the commandments. What's more, to save a life, your own or someone else's, you may ignore all the rules—life comes first. But there is an exception to this regulation: If you are to live by committing idolatry, adultery, or murder, then it is better to die.

Jews who attend synagogue services on the Sabbath and on holidays are never far from the Holocaust. Many synagogues have erected memorials to the six million Jews who were massacred in Europe in the dozen years between 1933 and 1945, when the Nazis reigned. Four times (on Passover, Shavuot, Yom Kippur, and Shmini Atzeret) observant Jews recite the *Yizkor* prayer, a memorial for loved ones. A separate, individual memorial called the *yahrzeit* also is observed on the anniversary of the decedent's death.

On the four holidays when the congregation as a whole

recites the moving words of the Yizkor prayer in memory of loved ones, many synagogues add a separate prayer for the six million martyrs. Although nearly a half-century has passed since the events of that period took place, there remains a feeling in the Jewish community that the missing third of the Jewish people always will be a reminder of the Jewish people's vulnerability.

Perhaps that is why it is so remarkable to recall that at the height of Nazi dominion in Europe, many of the Jews incarcerated in ghettos or camps retained their humanity in the face of unparalleled brutality. In the Warsaw Ghetto, for example, where hundreds of thousands of Jews had been compressed into a small, walled-in area surrounded by armed forces, where hunger, disease, and death became part of the daily routine, there existed a group of Jewish physicians who decided to keep careful notes on the effects of starvation—notes that might one day help other people someplace else. They reasoned, logically, that the medical notes they would maintain, describing their own reactions to slow starvation, would be extremely accurate. After all, they concluded, they themselves were the victims, and whose notes could be more accurate?

In the forests of Europe, there were bands of Jewish partisans who kept on fighting the Nazis and their collaborators. No one is quite sure how they managed to survive as long as they did. One of the reminders of that time is a song that they sang, in Yiddish, presumably around a lonely camp fire. They probably sang it softly so as not to be overheard, for as things turned out the Jewish partisans had to fight not only the Nazis but often also anti-Semitic Russian and Polish partisans.

The song that they sang, "Do Not Despair," appears in the new "Sim Shalom" prayerbook of the Conservative movement. It speaks for itself:

*Gevalt, Jews! Do not despair.*
*In the Holocaust the partisans sang.*
*Never say that we have come to journey's end*

*When days are dark and clouds upon the world descend.*
*Our past is a prelude; we are never at the end of the road.*
*God redeems the people Israel; He rebuilds Jerusalem.*
*In the Warsaw Ghetto,*
*Jews added an eleventh commandment:*
*Gevalt, Jews! You shall not despair.*
*We believe that justice and peace will reign.*
*God's splendor will then be seen in all humanity.*
*We believe in the sun even when it is not shining.*
*We believe in God even when He is silent.*
*We believe with perfect faith in the coming of the Messiah.*
*And though he tarry, as all of us have tarried,*
*Nevertheless—and truly—we believe.*
*Though we walk in the valley overshadowed by death,*
*We shall fear no harm for You are with us.*
*Gevalt, Jews! Do not despair.*
*Those who dwell in darkness will be bathed in light.*
*Ruthlessness and arrogance will cease to be.*
*The glory of humanity will be revealed.*
*The upright will rejoice, the pious celebrate in song.*
*There will be peace within our walls,*
*Serenity within our homes.*
*Hope in the Lord and be strong;*
*Take courage and hope in the Lord.*

Some historians maintain that the early Pilgrims who sought religious freedom in America patterned themselves on the biblical Hebrews whom they knew so well through their study of the Jewish Bible. Even the beautiful holiday of Thanksgiving, some insist, is modeled after the biblical Sukkot, the fall festival which marks the final harvest of the growing season.

One rabbi, Morris Silverman, saw precise similarities between America's founding texts and the ancient Jewish texts. The Declaration of Independence, for example, spoke that "all men are created equal . . . they are endowed by their Creator with certain inalienable rights," Compare these verses with

Malachi, chapter 2, verse 10: "Have we not all one father? Has not one God created us?"

In the Bill of Rights, Congress is specifically proscribed from making a "law respecting an establishment of religion, or prohibiting the free exercise thereof," which of course follows the spirit of the passage from Leviticus that was inscribed on the Liberty Bell: "Proclaim liberty throughout the land, for all of its inhabitants."

In the 1960s there was a worldwide rash of swastika daubings on synagogues and Jewish communal buildings throughout the world, including the United States. A Colorado daily published an editorial at the time entitled, "Jew, Go Home."

"Jew, go home!"

Well, now, this is nothing new. Never in the past have you ever taken this gentle suggestion to move on.

But suppose just this once you thought that this expression of a few sick people actually expressed the conviction of all the people in this wonderful land of ours, and all of you started to pack your bags and leave for parts unknown.

Just before you leave, would you do me a favor? Would you leave your formula to the Salk vaccine with me before you leave? You wouldn't be so heartless as to let my children contract polio.

And would you please leave your knack for government, and politics and persuasion, and literature, and good food, and fun, and love, and all those things? And would you please leave with me the secret to your drive to succeed, to make money? I need more.

And please have pity on us, please show us the secret of how to develop such geniuses as Einstein, Steinmetz and oh so many others who have helped us all. After all, we owe you most of the A-bomb, most of our rocket research, and perhaps the fact that we are alive today instead of looking up from our chains and from our graves to see an aging, happy Hitler driving slowly by in one of our Cadillacs.

On your way out, Jews, will you do me just one more favor?

Will you please drive by my house and pick me up too?

I'm just not sure I could live well in a land where you weren't around to give us as much as you have given us.

If you ever have to leave, love goes with you, democracy goes with you, everything I and all my buddies fought for in World War II goes with you, and God goes with you.

Just pull up in front of my house, slow down and honk, because so help me, I'm going with you, too.

# 7. JEWISH ETHICS

*Passing ethical values from generation to genera-
tion: no easy task . . . Thousand years ago,
Maimonides advised his children how to conduct
their lives, stressing wisdom, humility, sanctity . . .
Rigid versus flexible Jewish viewpoints.*

THROUGH THE AGES PARENTS HAVE SOUGHT TO PASS DOWN
to their children values that would enhance the younger generation's future life. This has been no easy task, to put it mildly.
History has shown that the rebellion against the fathers by the
teens is not a new phenomenon. Even the Passover Haggadah
speaks of a "rebellious son."

There is a story of David Ben Gurion, Israel's first prime
minister and the acknowledged architect of the Jewish state.
B. G., as he was usually called, and his wife, Paula, had one
son, Amos, and two daughters. The Ben Gurions were by no
means observant Jews in the narrow sense, although the Israeli
leader spent a lifetime studying the Bible, alone and under the
tutelage of some of Israel's leading rabbis and scholars. However, when his son informed him that he planned to get

married, and that the young lady in question was an English Gentile, Ben Gurion knew anguish.

What to do? What he did, after the first shock wore off, was send the future bride a copy of the Jewish Bible, together with a long, warm letter, wishing the couple well and inviting her to convert to Judaism. In time, she did, and everything worked out well.

Nonetheless, Jewish parents (and grandparents) today still worry about the problem of how to explain to their children the basic precepts of Judaism and the compelling reasons why they should decide to live a committed, full Jewish life. In many cases, the problem is made more difficult by the fact that a good part of the adult Jewish population in the United States, while successful, is sometimes less formally educated than their sons and daughters. This makes for a difficult intergenerational gap.

The problem is not new. Centuries ago, Jewish scholars in Europe evolved a way of speaking to the next generation through a device called an "ethical will"—a kind of last message to be read after the parents (usually the father) had passed on, and which had nothing to do with any kind of other will that disposed of property.

Maimonides, one of the greatest Jewish personalities of all time, lived nearly one thousand years ago. He was a master scholar and commentator, an outstanding physician, and a communal leader and major philosopher. Before his passing he wrote:

> Thus far hath the Lord blessed and preserved me, granting unto me wisdom beyond my fellows, and enabling me to distinguish between good and evil. My end is in His hand, and He hath made me conscious of it, though I know not how long nor how short-lived am I. Therefore hath His love stirred me to admonish the children whom He hath graciously bestowed on me, that they may observe the way of the Lord.
>
> I would teach them what He hath taught me, bequeath to

them the heritage which He gave me, before He calls me away, and His Glory gather me in.

Hear me, my children! Blessed be ye of the Lord, who made heaven and earth, with blessing of heaven above. . . . Be strong and show yourselves men. Fear the Lord, the God of your father, the God of Abraham, Isaac and Jacob; and serve Him with a perfect heart, from fear and from love. Fear restrains from sin, and love stimulates virtue. . . . He who leads a good life finds good even in this world. . . . I entreat you to recognize the excellency of light over darkness. Reject death and evil, choose life and good, for the free choice is given to you! Accustom yourselves to habitual goodness, for habit and character are closely interwoven, habit becoming as it were second nature. . . . When I bid you to care for your bodily and moral welfare, my purpose is to open for you the gates of heaven! Conduct yourselves with gravity and decency; avoid association with the wanton, sit not in the streets, sport not with the young, for the fruit thereof is evil.

Be found in the company of the great and learned, but behave modestly in their presence. . . . Open the ears of your heart to listen and to understand their words, and what they praise and blame. Weigh their opinions and thus you will be set in the right way. Guard your tongue from wearying them, measure your words with judgment, for the more your words, the more your errors. . . . Ponder well over every word before you utter it, for you cannot recall it afterwards.

Love wisdom. Be found on the threshhold of the wise, those that learn and those that teach. There obtain your recreation, there take delight in hearing discourse of science and morals, as well as the new thoughts and ingenious arguments of the students.

Emulate those who seek knowledge, despise those who have no intellectual curiosity. Whether you ask a question or answer one, speak without haste or obscurity, softly and without stammering. . . . Behave as one who wishes to learn and to discover the truth, not as one whose aim is to dispute and win a wordy victory.

Love truth and righteousness, and cleave to them. . . . hate falsehood and injustice, lust not after their dainties, for such happiness is built on sand. Disdain reservations, subterfuges, tricks, sharp practices and evasions. Woe to him that builds his house thereon! Live in sincerity, integrity, innocence! Touch not that which is not yours, be it a small matter or great. . . . Flee from doubtful possessions, treat them as the property of others. . . . Be pitiful to the poor and the sorrow-stricken. See to it that they share your joys.

Condemn idleness, loathe ease, for these corrupt the body and lead to all manner of poverty and perversity, in pocket and in conversation. . . . Hate dissension and flee from it. Recognize the worth of forbearance. Sanctify yourselves and be holy in the eyes of your enemies. . . . Behave with humility, for it is the ladder to the topmost heights. The master of the prophets, Moses, was not so distinguished in Scripture for any of his qualities as for his virtue of humility. . . .

Eat that you may live; place a ban on excess. . . . Enjoy life in the company of your friends and the wife of your young manhood. Remember the warnings of Scripture against unchastity. Never excite desire, and when in the course of nature it comes upon you, satisfy it in the manner ordained by moral rule, to raise up offspring, and to perpetuate the human race.

Though you should not be dominated by your wives or reveal to them secrets placed in your keeping, you must honor your wives, for they are your honor. Serve those who love you, and those near unto you, with your person and your substance, according to the good hand of the Lord upon you. But take heed lest you serve them with your soul, for that is the divine portion.

Are Maimonides' words of a millenium ago still relevant and meaningful today? I think so. The human condition has not really changed all that much in all that time.

There is a great deal of discussion today within the Jewish community about the need for unity. People not familiar with Jewish history or with the inner workings of the organized Jewish community may fail to understand that the dissension they read about from time to time is a phenomenon of our hectic time, and not an omen of the swift decline of the Jewish people. There are great and weighty problems within the Jewish people, but I believe the Cassandras predicting a tragic end to our existence are wrong.

A study of the history of the Jewish people will demonstrate that there almost always has been a split within the community. Millenia ago there were two camps of Jews—the Pharisees and the Sadducees, the latter shunning the oral law and rabbinical interpretation and insisting on a literal reading and understanding of the Bible. Through the centuries there were differing interpretations of Talmudic laws and rulings.

The schools of Hillel and Shammai might be said to symbolize two differing approaches to Judaism, the latter representing a rigid interpretation and the former a far more lenient view. (In most advanced classes in yeshivas, both views are studied to this day, even though one or the other decision has been accepted as binding—pretty much like lawyers who study a decision by the Supreme Court, and who wish to know both the final decision arrived at and the views of the dissenting justices).

There are liturgical differences between the Ashkenazi and Sephardic Jews (the latter are Jews descended from Iberia and the countries bordering on the Mediterranean, while the former are Jews whose forebears lived in central, eastern, and later western Europe). In fact, until the Second World War, a marriage between an Ashkenazi and a Sephardic Jew usually was opposed by the respective parents, or at the least it was considered socially undesirable. (That particular notion has almost totally disappeared. Indeed, the Israelis today like to joke about the fact that more and more of their young people are "intermarrying"—the percentage of Ashkenazi-Sephardic marriages continues to rise each year, and today stands about thirty percent. Interestingly, one Israeli medical researcher encourages these marriages, maintaining that such unions will go far to wipe out Jewish genetic diseases that are usually passed on from one generation to another in marriages within a narrow section of the Jewish community.)

Although the number of Ashkenazi Jews in the United States is far greater than the Sephardic total, the number of Sephardic Jews in Israel (together with those Jews who came from Islamic countries) outnumbers the Ashkenazim by fifty-five to forty-five percent. The earliest Jewish settlers in the Americas almost all were Sephardic Jews. Some of the greatest Jewish leaders and philosophers were Sephardic—for example, Maimonides, Judah Halevi, Ibn-Ezra, Luzzato, and many others.

There were Jewish sects who broke away from the mainstream of the Jewish people because of fundamental differences in interpreting the Bible. Beginning in the eighth century, a group calling itself the Karaites insisted on eliminating all rabbinical rulings and interpretations of the Bible, while their opposites, the Rabbanites, taught that the rabbinical commentaries and the oral law as a whole were equal to the Torah itself. Modern Jewish people worldwide are descended from the Rabbanites. There still exist tiny pockets of Karaite Jews in various parts of the world.

One of the greatest schisms within the community began in the eighteenth century in the wake of the growth and development of the Hassidic movement. The Hassidim, who initially frowned on study in favor of song and dance, were opposed by the *Mitnagdim,* the classical students of lifelong Judaic study, whose *yeshivot* proliferated throughout the Baltic states, Russia, and Poland. In 1781 the Jewish leaders of East European communities went so far as to formally excommunicate the Hassidim, claiming that they had "separated themselves from the community, (making) separate customs and sinful laws. They take apart the Torah and encourage chaos." Marriages between Hassidim and Mitnagdim were banned; the Hassidim fought back, burning the books and pamphlets published by the Mitnagdim. It was a bitter internecine fight that lasted for many years. Today, although there certainly are disagreements and disputes between various Hassidic groups and the majority non-Hassidic Jewish community, there is at the very least a truce between them on issues that could threaten to divide the community.

However, there are exceptions. Israel has varying types of Orthodox Jewish communities, and while most Israelis, observant and nonobservant alike, get along well, there also are extremists whose actions often make news. These are the fundamentalists who throw stones at Jews seen driving on the Sabbath and set fire to advertising posters at bus stops because they think the bikini-clad models are immodest in their dress.

In more recent times, in the last century, there were some Orthodox Jews who opposed the Zionist movement because they thought that Jews in exile should continue to wait for the arrival of the Messiah—and since early Zionist leaders like Herzl, Weizmann, and Ben Gurion were not observant Jews, they could not be the long-awaited Messiah. However, most Orthodox Jews changed their minds as conditions in the world changed. (There still remains, however, a tiny number of Jews, living both in Israel and in the U.S., who oppose Israel, insisting that God will send the Messiah to redeem the Jewish people when He is ready.)

In America, up until the rise of Nazism and the outbreak of the Second World War, the Reform movement was largely anti-Zionist. One of the early founders of the American Reform movement, Rabbi Isaac Mayer Wise, helped to establish a Reform rabbinical seminary in Cincinnati. He said at the time: "Cincinnati is our new Zion." Today, however, there is virtually no difference in the degree of support that American Jews of all religious groupings extend to Israel. In fact, there are even *kibbutzim*—collective, communal farming communities in Israel—that are operated by Reform Jewish immigrants from the U.S.

Perhaps this historic chasm within Jewry accounts for the popular story that is told about a Jew who was rescued from an island in the South Pacific after many years. His rescuers noted that there were two synagogues on the small island, and asked if there were other Jews living there. "Oh, no," he replied. He pointed to the nearer of the two and said: "That's my *shul*, that's where I go to pray. The other one I never set foot in!"

Although most Jews in all parts of the world feel comfortable and at home in virtually any synagogue anywhere, there are some Jews who look askance at services where an organ may be heard playing in the background or where some of the male worshipers pray with their heads uncovered. Then there are other worshipers, accustomed to being seated alongside their spouses, who find the separation of the sexes in traditional synagogues unacceptable.

Not so long ago, the story goes, Elizabeth Taylor, who converted to Judaism when she married Mike Todd, was in Paris during the ten-day High Holy Days. She was married at the time to Richard Burton, who of course was a Christian. She decided she wanted to attend services on Yom Kippur, and persuaded her husband to join her. When the two approached the synagogue, they immediately were recognized, and were warmly welcomed. But when the ushers insisted that Burton had to be seated downstairs with the men, and Elizabeth Taylor upstairs with the women, she purportedly objected loudly and strenuously but to no avail. She went upstairs to join the other women.

I have been a worshiper in two Parisian synagogues. Once was on the eve of Purim, which celebrates the ancient rescue of the Persian Jewish community and when the story of the festival is read aloud in the synagogue. The other time was at a Sabbath morning service in a Reform-oriented service. On Purim eve, when it is customary to wear costumes and even to imbibe until one is a little tipsy, I was delighted to see the ushers walking around wearing what I thought were silly Napoleonic hats—until I was informed that I was in Paris, and that those historic hats were not considered offbeat.

At the Sabbath morning service, where I was searched and my wife's purse was checked (there had been a bombing a year earlier and the French gendarmes were taking no chances), I was thrilled to realize that I was able to follow, partially anyway, the rabbi's carefully enunciated French sermon. He clearly spoke of "le bon Dieu" and the prayer book in my hands had the ancient Hebrew words translated into French, rather than English, as I was accustomed to at home.

One of the basic precepts of Judaism is known as *ahavath yisrael*, love for the people of Israel. It takes a little effort to extend to a fellow Jew a sense of love and companionship, rather than to pressure him into affiliating with one or another Jewish grouping.

The Lubavitch Hassidim, whose members often can be seen in the larger metropolitan areas urging women to bless the Sabbath eve candles and encouraging men to step into their parked vans to pray with *tallit* and *tefillin*, have a saying that I enjoy. One has to remember that in their thinking, the Messiah will arrive to redeem the world when Jews without exception will observe the Sabbath totally and perfectly. They do not throw rocks at Sabbath drivers. They like to encourage Jews to become more observant of their own free will. When pointing to a Jew who may be walking down the street on the Sabbath carrying a tennis racket and on his way to play instead of going to religious services, the Lubavitch Hassid will say: *Er iz noch nisht frum.* Translation: "He is not yet a religious person." It is a benign, noncoercive, positive approach, certainly to be preferred to the extremist rock throwers, whether or not one supports the Lubavitch or any other Hassidic group.

Rabbi Shlomo Riskin, a charismatic young rabbi who established a very successful synagogue catering largely to young people in the shadow of Lincoln Center in New York City, and who now lives in a small town a few miles from Jerusalem, likes to describe his own custom on Sabbath morning when he returns home from services. When he passes a fellow townsman or a neighbor seated at the wheel of his car, waiting for the light to change, he rushes over, extends his hand, and wishes the driver a Shabbat Shalom, a peaceful Sabbath. He does this not to make him feel guilty, Riskin explains, but to show him that "we are both Jews, both descendants of the patriarchs," and that brotherly love and devotion must transcend everything else.

The fact is that in the United States today, and I believe the same thing applies in Israel, France, England, and wherever there are large Jewish communities, the main issue confronting the Jewish people is relevance.

How do we make Jewish life, no matter how one understands that term, become so attractive, meaningful, and enjoyable in the 1990s to hundreds of thousands of young, educated, and sophisticated Jews?

These now are generations of the post-Holocaust years and the nuclear threat age, of a largely secular world where formal religious practice often is seen as antiquated and outdated.

There is however, according to all religious thinkers of the West, the East, and also of the more primitive cultures, a common thread of uncertainty that runs through all civilizations, peoples, and through all history. People are asking, silently or vocally: What is life all about? Is there an afterlife? Are the just rewarded and the unjust punished? What is it that we strive for, and then lose quickly to the grim reaper? To put it another way, What does Judaism teach us about life? To put it crassly, What's in it for me? Why should I lead a "Jewish life?"

# 8. PERSECUTION OF THE JEWS

*Why so much hatred against Jews? Some said because Jews prick conscience of people; others said Jews are hated for their virtues, not vices . . . Tolstoy said Jews were "pioneers of civilization and liberty" . . . Meeting Judaism halfway.*

IF IT IS TRUE THAT THE WORLD FACES MAJOR PROBLEMS that threaten the very future of the planet, is it not then just a little parochial to insist on maintaining a strictly Jewish identity? Shouldn't intelligent people band together to resolve the problems of nuclear arms, AIDS, drugs, rampant crime, growing poverty, fundamentalist religion that often is coupled with brainwashing, cultic movements, cancer, heart disease, and on and on and on?

There are many possible answers to this basic question. Among them: Being Jewish means caring deeply about all people and all issues confronting humanity. It is not by any stretch of the imagination a narrow, selfish religion. Being Jewish means, in the words of Tolstoy, "(being) the religious source, spring and fountain out of which all the rest of the peoples have drawn their beliefs and their religions."

Tolstoy's description of the Jew as "the pioneer of liberty" is interesting. The Jew also is seen as

> the pioneer of civilization—ignorance was condemned in olden Palestine even more than it is today in civilized Europe. In those wild and barbarous days, when neither the life nor the death of anyone counted for anything at all, Rabbi Akiba did not refrain from expressing himself openly against capital punishment.

Tolstoy noted that Moses taught his people to "love the stranger and sojourner" in those "savage times when the principal ambition of the races and nations consisted of crushing and enslaving one another." The Jew, Tolstoy added, is the

> emblem of eternity. He whom neither fire nor sword nor inquisition was able to wipe off the face of the earth, he who was the first to produce the oracles of God, he who has been for so long a guardian of prophecy, and who transmitted it to the rest of the world—such a nation cannot be destroyed. The Jew is everlasting, as is eternity itself.

What kind of people are Jews, according to Jewish sources? Over the centuries the descriptions have come down from profound thinkers, careful scholars, and the man in the street. "Jews are first to feel universal disaster or joy," said Simeon ben Lakish a long time ago. "The Torah was given to the Jews because they are impetuous" and need discipline, was the view of Talmudic sage Rabbi Meir. The historian Graetz concluded that "thinking became just as characteristic a feature of the Jews as suffering." The historian Dubnow adduced that the "spiritual discipline of the school came to mean for the Jew what military discipline is for other nations." "If the Jews are not prophets," Hillel said a long time ago, "then they are the sons of prophets."

So, why so much hate against Jews? Herzl said it was "for

his virtues not his vices that the Jew is hated." Nearly a century ago American scholar E. G. Hirsch gave his explanation: "The Jew is an irritant that brings forever to the conscience of the people their shortcomings. This is the cause of hatred against the Jew."

The original question persists: Why be Jewish? Is it to be hated, or to take pride in the fact that one is the descendant of prophets, of a great people who brought religion to the world? Are these ample reasons? I don't think so.

A person who is born Jewish and knows that being Jewish can be a lifelong source of joy, guidance, and a way of life for children who follow has no problem. He is a proud, committed Jew. The same may be said of a person who comes to Judaism late in life, who is a *baal teshuva*, a "new-born Jew," for whom learning the minutest detail of Jewish law and lore becomes an obsession—that person has no problem. Nor has the "Jew by choice," the convert who has studied, undergone formal conversion, and feels comfortable in the newly adopted faith.

But what of the large numbers in between those totally committed to Judaism and those who are on the fringes of the Jewish people? Too many of these latter associate Judaism and Jewish life with the past, with their parents and/or grandparents, with the old country, with the declining influence of religion. Mind you, they may very well have a positive attitude towards being Jewish, knowing that it is a way of life that has made enormous contributions to society and civilization for millenia. They also may feel strongly that they do not want to see Hitler achieve a posthumous victory, which is precisely what will happen if large numbers of Jews in the West slowly but steadily move along the road of intermarriage and assimilation and gradually disappear from the Jewish community.

Will it mean anything to point out to such young people, often very educated and knowledgeable people, that of the three great ancient civilizations that have come down to us in the West—Greece, Rome and Israel—it is only the Jewish

people's goals that remain as strong and as valid today as they
did thousands of years ago?

The Greeks gave the world art, science, literature, philosophy, and our political code. But Greece had contempt for the
poor and the weak and felt no need for a just, merciful God.
Rome on the other hand learned to use force to subjugate any
people's quest for political, religious, or cultural freedom. But
the ancient Jews burned with anger over the world's abuses of
the impoverished and the downtrodden. They burn with the
same fire today. As the historian Renan wrote:

> The prophets were fanatics in the cause of social justice and loudly
> proclaimed that if the world was not just, or capable of becoming
> so, it had better be destroyed—a view that, if utterly wrong, led to
> deeds of heroism and brought about a grand awakening of the
> forces of humanity.

The French Jewish leader, Bernard Lazare, once said that
being Jewish "is the least difficult way of being truly human."

Inez Lowdermilk, who lived for many years in Palestine/
Israel with her husband, Walter, the distinguished agricultural
scientist who did so much to restore the Holy Land's produc-
tivity, liked to point to the sources of Western civilization and
note how "they reach back to Jewish roots." Ethics and the
Ten Commandments came from the Jewish people, she liked
to say, as well as the Bible itself. "The Jews taught us to be
monotheistic and worship one God, and their God became
our God," she wrote.

> The Law of Moses has been a basis for legal systems of the rest of
> the world. . . . The Hebrew prophets proclaimed the ideals for a
> righteous, just social order that we have not yet begun to reach.
> They demanded the right of free speech and insisted that individ-
> uals be responsible for their own actions.
>      The greatest teacher of all the ages was a Jew—Jesus of
> Nazareth. He taught the fatherhood of God, the brotherhood of

man, and that we should do unto others as we would have others do unto us. It is the saddest blot on our Western history that we, as Christian nations, have failed so miserably in living up to the teachings of this great law.

Our own America was built from a blueprint provided by the ancient Jews. Thomas Jefferson was asked how he knew how to create, out of thirteen colonies, a democratic republic when there never was one before. Jefferson answered, "Why, we went to the first Jewish Commonwealth as described by Moses in the wilderness . . . and we copied the format."

Moses said, "Choose ye wise men from among you to represent you," and that's what we have done with the Supreme Court, the Senate and the Congress. The Jews set a precedent for the equality that Western women are still striving for. Moses gave extra dignity to women and girls; the prophets also dignified women.

Jews number among our greatest scientists, writers, scholars, and physicians. They have developed serums to do away with the curse of polio and the blindness of trachoma. . . . During the years I, as a Christian, lived in the Holy Land, I witnessed Israel's treatment of defeated Arab enemies. No nation in history has been so humane. In none of her wars has Israel gloated, looted, or raped. I saw how Israelis provided bread and milk for besieged Arabs, provided health care for Arab children to fight against polio and trachoma, assisted Arabs with agricultural services, and paid Arab farmers the same prices that Jewish farmers received for crops.

When Christians remember that their roots and historic memories are tied to the Holy Land, we will understand why it is crucial for us to help Israel to be a strong, independent democracy in the Middle East.

Does being Jewish and living a Jewish life bring happiness? Look at some of the biblical texts that have wrestled with the problem: Proverbs says that people who support wisdom are happy. Psalms notes that people who trust in God are happy; elsewhere the psalmist asserts that people who do not commit sins or associate with sinners are happy. Psalms also notes that people who practice justice or who are concerned about the poor are happy people. Isaiah maintains that people who observe the Sabbath are happy.

Early in this century Montefiore wrote that "the best way to attain happiness is not to seek it." Live, in other words, a full, productive, shared life, and *ipso facto* happiness will follow.

The American ideal of life, liberty, and the pursuit of happiness differs from the Jewish view. Life and liberty, yes, Judaism is in full agreement. As for happiness, Judaism seems to be saying to us, it will ensue if you lead a good life filled with kindness, justice, and acts of lovingkindness.

When the ancient Israelites stood at Mount Sinai, tradition tells us, and they were proferred the Torah, their response was *naaseh v'nishma*—we will do these things, and we will obey. In other words, they did not really understand the meaning or the purposes of the rules that were being set before them, but they were ready to perform the deeds that were required, and in so doing they would be obeying God's law. This in turn would bring about a time of joy and fulfillment.

In the overwhelming majority of cases I have seen, Jews who add or expand their "Jewish dimension" are happier, more fulfilled, serene, and satisfied.

A person can live a good, moral life and never step into a synagogue or participate in a Jewish welfare or educational program, but it's hard, and it's a lonely lifestyle. Members of synagogues, Jewish organizations, and community centers often are busy doing things for others and walking away from their chores with a marvelous sense of achievement.

There are members of the synagogue to which I belong who are not all that comfortable at prayer services or hearing the rabbi lecture on some aspect of Judaism. They remain members year in and year out, and one sees them working hard, long hours at fund-raising bazaars, providing support for the synagogue and deriving a great measure of support and satisfaction for themselves.

I also have seen Jewish businessmen, and industrialists,

often men in their late sixties or seventies, who gravitated toward organizations that supported economic or educational programs in Israel. These were men accustomed to directing vast enterprises with thousands of employees, and here they were, crowded into a small room, munching on a sandwich after a full day's work and discussing ways and means of advancing the work of a particular group. The organization, for them, has become a kind of temple and the work a form of worship. Working for a good cause, in this case a Jewish cause, had brought these older American Jews a sense of achievement that often eluded them, no matter how many millions they had succeeded in amassing during their lives. Doing for others, helping to "correct the world" a little—this ancient Jewish motif has remained firmly imbedded in the hearts and minds of these people.

Happily, this same strong motivation remains deeply entrenched. Thousands of Jews of all ages and economic levels continue to give of themselves and their wealth to a wide gamut of causes. It is part of being Jewish.

Being part of the organized Jewish community; taking part in religious services and/or attending classes; helping a person in need; providing funds for a cause or community; observing the Sabbath and the holidays; learning more and more about the Jewish heritage through books, newspapers and magazines, art, film, music; and visiting Israel and points of Jewish interest both in the U.S. and overseas all can heighten your Jewish awareness. They can fill a spiritual/cultural/religious void, provide a sense of community and continuity, and, yes, bring deeper happiness and fulfillment.

But you still have to work at it. You cannot sit back and just let it come to you. You have to go out and, at the least, meet Jewish life halfway.

# 9. JEWISH ILLITERACY

*"Jewish illiteracy" in America is widespread . . . Edward G. Robinson sings synagogue hymn . . . Nazi's son is now a bearded, orthodox rabbi in Israel . . . Jews take on traits of countries in which they have lived for centuries.*

ALTHOUGH BY AND LARGE JEWISH MEN, WOMEN, AND CHIL-dren form a very educated community, it is one of the greatest ironies that when it comes to specifically Judaic knowledge, large portions of the younger and middle-aged generations of contemporary Jews are "Jewishly illiterate."

At a Sabbath synagogue service, it is not uncommon for a member of the bar or bat mitzvah party—a relative or friend—to be honored by being called to the Torah. That's when the fun begins. Often the honoree in question—and he could be a professor with a doctorate, a trained physician, or a lawyer—cannot read Hebrew, so that when he is required to pronounce the proper blessing, he must rely on the English transliteration that discreetly is placed before him. Sometimes those poor, ancient syllables are so distorted they sound like a lost language of antiquity.

But wait, we're not through yet. It is customary for the person called to the Torah to be blessed, and all he needs to do is to convey his Hebrew name to the *gabbai*, or the Torah reader's aide.

"What is your name?" the *gabbai* will ask softly.

"Abraham Greenberg," the honoree responds.

"No, no, your Hebrew name, and your father's."

A look of consternation sweeps over the guest's face. "My Hebrew name . . ." he repeats, already looking lost.

"It's all right, your Hebrew name is *Avraham*, it's almost the same as Abraham. What about your father's name?"

"Maurice. His name was Maurice Greenberg. I don't know his Hebrew name, I'm sorry."

"Try to remember—was it Moshe? Meir? Menashe?"

"I'm sorry, I don't know. He never told me."

"All right, we'll make it Moshe." The *gabbai* then proceeds to pronounce the traditional blessing for the honoree hoping the name he has just affixed to the perplexed visitor at his side is correct.

The state of "Jewish illiteracy" in the Western world already is at a critical point. It is fair to say that the vast American Jewish community is unevenly divided between an over-whelming majority that is painfully ignorant about the Jewish heritage and the smaller minority that is knowledgeable to a lesser or larger part.

The "People of the Book" for whom learning and education have been fundamental milestones of life for millennia, ap-proach the year 2000 with great numbers of Jews who are ignorant of their history, religious heritage, Jewish precepts and teachings, Hebrew, customs and ceremonies—in short, their very long roots.

The paucity of Jewish knowledge is astounding. While many modern Jews know that Freud was Jewish and that Marx came from Jewish roots, painfully few can say for sure who Rashi was, or Maimonides, or even in our own day, Brandeis. (Brandeis was America's first Jewish member of the U.S. Supreme Court; although he came from a nonobservant family, he became the leading Zionist figure in the U.S. as well as an advisor to presidents. Maimonides was a physician, scholar, rabbi and philosopher whose seminal works continue to be studied to this day. He lived most of his life in Egypt, until his death in 1204. Rashi, who is probably the principal commentator and interpreter of the Bible and Talmud, lived in a small French community near Mainz and Worms in the eleventh century.)

To demonstrate the depth of Jewish ignorance, rabbis like to tell the story of a congregant who kept on pestering his rabbi for a favor—to make him a *kohen*. A little explanation is needed here. In Jewish life there are three religious classifications, the highest being the "kohen" or priest, the second highest, the "levi" or levite, and the third encompasses everyone else and is known as "Yisrael," Israel or just plain folks. When someone is called to the Torah on Sabbath morning or on a holiday, the kohen goes first, the levite second, and after that everybody else follows. Now how do you get to be a kohen or a levite? You inherit the honor from your father, and he from his father, and so on all the way back.

Here was this congregant, pestering the rabbi about making him a kohen and increasing the amount of money he pledged to donate to the synagogue if only the rabbi would accede to his request.

Finally, in exasperation, after the rabbi had told his congregant that he could not change his standing no matter how much money he was willing to contribute, he asked the man why it was so important for him to become a kohen.

"Well, don't you see, rabbi?" the gentleman answered. "My

father was a kohen, and my grandfather, and I'd like to be one, too." He simply was too uninformed to know that he was a kohen, thanks to his father.

There is a marvelous scene in the movie *Exodus* in which Paul Newman stars as the intrepid hero Ari Ben-Canaan. At one point, wearing a stolen British military uniform, he poses as a British officer, and asks a fellow officer, a rabid anti-Semite, to help remove a cinder from his eye. As he struggles to clear Newman's eye, the Britisher spouts off about Jews. "You can always tell them apart, you can smell them," he insists. At which point Newman, the cinder gone, in his best imitation British accent, agrees with the English officer, and then departs to pull off another rescue operation of detained Jews.

Who are the Jews? One brief stroll through Tel Aviv, or for that matter a visit to a synagogue in an American city, will wipe out any vestigial ideas about the so-called Jewish look. Because of centuries of living among Slavs in eastern Europe and Balts in the states bordering the Baltic Sea, Jews who originate in that part of the world look like Russians, Poles, Lithuanians, *et al.*

The Jews who remained a more or less closed community, like the Jews of Yemen, Iraq, or Ethiopia, over a period of time took on the physical characteristics of those countries. And, one must add, very often they also absorbed the national traits of their host countries. Thus, an English Jew who settles in Israel today usually is "very English" while a Jew who arrives as an immigrant from Argentina generally brings with him the cultural values of South America.

One of the great religious leaders of this generation is the rebbe of the Lubavitch movement, Rabbi Menachem Schneersohn. He is, of course, never shown without a head covering, usually a conservative fedora. His is a gentle, scholarly, even sensitive face. But take away the hat, remove the full beard, and you have a prototypical, husky Russian peasant. One will find among Russian Jews traces of the physiognomy of Tatars and other non-Jews. Somewhere, during the course of centuries, there were Jewish girls who were raped or who had liaisons with Gentile neighbors, and this factor, multiplied over centuries and many locales, produced a broad gamut of untypical "Jewish looks." The Museum of the Jewish Diaspora in Tel Aviv—a must see for any visitor—has a series of illuminated Jewish faces that in moments shatters all misconceptions about the so-called Jewish look.

To illustrate the far-reaching nature of this phenomenon, there is the remarkable story of a rabbi now living and working in Israel. To look at him is to see a bearded, fortyish man, a *yarmulke* firmly planted on his head. His Hebrew is flawless, his English excellent, and his eyes sparkle and twinkle when he speaks. He is married to a sabra—a native-born Israeli—and photos of his children prominently are displayed.

So what makes him special? Only the fact that he was born a German Christian, the son of a man who supported Hitler. As a young man he went out into the world seeking understanding and knowledge. At one point he decided to convert and become Jewish, which he did in a Reform ceremony. Later, as he seemed to reach even deeper into his soul, he underwent another conversion ceremony with an Orthodox rabbi and eventually was ordained as an Orthodox rabbi.

The moral seems clear: Being born Jewish is an accident of birth. For the born Jew or for the "Jew by choice," Judaism means a lifelong commitment to good works and to study. Continual Jewish learning is an integral part of being Jewish.

That is why the great Jewish text, "Ethics of the Fathers," a compilation of rabbinical adages and concepts assembled from Talmudic sources, cautions: "Say not when I have leisure I will study; you may not have leisure. . . . Make your study of Torah a fixed engagement."

The question repeats itself. Who are the Jews? The historian Cecil Roth, in his volume *The Jewish Contribution to Civilization,* lists long rosters of Jews who have made enormous strides in many different fields of endeavor. The sixteen-volume *Encyclopedia Judaica* lists thousands of Jews over the centuries who have made notable contributions to society.

Probably every person has his own small list of Jewish men and women who have had a positive Jewish influence on them. Parents, grandparents, teachers, a rabbi, a neighbor, a friend—it often was something that was taught or said or demonstrated that made a lasting impression on a young, malleable person.

My own parents, grandparents, and teachers were excellent role models. I learned integrity, honesty, and a sense of caring from them all. Being Jewish was part of our daily lives; the synagogue was an extension of home and the congregants part of an extended family. But we were recent immigrants to America and there remained a gnawing question for years at the back of one's mind: How do "real Americans"—Jews who were firmly rooted, spoke without accents, and were respected by their Gentile friends and neighbors—act vis-à-vis their Jewish backgrounds?

I remember two incidents that helped me realize that being a committed Jew did not have to interfere with one's life one iota. I was in a room with actor Edward G. Robinson, who had just finished taping a radio commercial for the United Jewish Appeal. He was at the zenith of his international fame at the time; his work finished, he was now ready to relax. There was a piano in the room. He asked if anyone could play and a volunteer approached the piano.

"What'll it be, Eddie?" he asked.

The actor smiled his impish smile, which had been seen by millions and millions of people throughout the world.

"Do you know 'Adon Olam'?" he asked.

The pianist began to play, we gathered around Robinson,

and together we all sang "Adon Olam," the traditional closing hymn of the Sabbath morning synagogue service.

On another occasion, Jack Benny and his manager were seated in the same room with me, and the famed performer must have been in a nostalgic mood.

"You know," he said to me, when he learned that I knew Hebrew, "I wish to hell I could still remember how to write my name in Hebrew. I could do it at my bar mitzvah."

High in a hotel room in Houston, Texas, on a quiet Saturday night, I sat with Benny and showed him how his name looked in the ancient script. He folded the piece of paper into his wallet, genuinely pleased.

Who are the Jews? I think of two other Jews. One, a survivor of World War I, found himself in a tiny cabin in Poland in 1919, desperately huddling near a stove to keep warm, an old blanket wrapped around him. On the rough table in the corner he saw two sardine cans, the last remaining food that had been sent to him and other needy Polish Jews by the Joint Distribution Committee in New York. He wondered what he would eat after the sardines were consumed.

For the first time he became aware of the wrapping paper in which the cans were shipped—a months-old copy of the popular New York Yiddish daily, the *Forward*. Languidly he began to read, and suddenly he spotted a small ad that seemed to jump out of the page. A store on the Lower East Side was offering heavy winter underwear at reduced prices. *Oh,* he thought, *could I use a pair of those!* They covered the body completely, from the neck to the soles of the feet. *I would be able to work,* he thought, *if I weren't so cold all the time.*

The youngish Polish Jew, his ancient blanket still wrapped around him, found paper and pencil and wrote to the owner of the store. He explained how he came across his name, about the ad, and about his own circumstances. He added that he was embarrassed to ask, but if his situation were not so desperate, he wouldn't do so. One pair of the underwear, he said in the letter, could make all the difference in one poor Jew's life.

The letter was sent. In six weeks a package arrived in the small Polish village, and when it was opened, the recipient found two pairs of the Long John underwear, and tucked into the pocket of one pair was a $100 bill with a brief note: "Dear Sir. Received your letter, which brought tears to my eyes and made me remember how poor I was not so many years ago. Enclosed are two pairs. I hope the money will give you a fresh start. God bless you."

The money enabled the young Polish Jew to start a small retail business. Gradually, his lot in life improved. He married, children began to arrive, and at least once a year he and his distant benefactor in New York exchanged greetings, usually for the Jewish New Year. It was hard to believe that ten years had passed when, one cold December in 1929, the Polish Jew received an urgent letter from New York.

> My dear friend. I cannot believe what is happening here. They call it a crash, a depression. All I know is that the world has turned upside down for me. Nobody comes in to buy, I have no money to pay my bills, I worry day and night how I will feed my family. If it is possible, could you return the $100 I sent you ten years ago? I would appreciate it very much.

The Polish Jew had not heard of any depression, and the worldwide economic slide had apparently not yet touched Poland. He approached some of his friends, told them about his former benefactor's letter and about his new situation, and together with his own money put together a cable transmission of six hundred dollars, addressed to his New York co-religionist.

The years rolled on. Slowly, the world's economy improved. In the middle 1930s the two Jews began to write more frequently to each other about a new menace: the rise of Nazism in Germany. The American Jew urged his friend to leave Poland, promising to help him as much as he could. In

1936 the Polish Jew left Poland for Palestine with his family, and thus avoided becoming an additional statistic in the Holocaust.

The two men continued to correspond. Finally, in the late 1960s, they met for the first time in Tel Aviv, when the New Yorker paid his first visit to Israel. It was an emotional meeting, of course—like two long-lost brothers who had finally been reunited.

Although neither man was an especially learned Jew, they both knew—from their parents, studies, and the sacred words of the Jewish texts—"He who saves a life, it is as though he saved the world."

Being Jewish means not only caring and compassionate concern about the other fellow, but also acting on the need. Making right a wrong. Correcting the world.

# Part Two: **HOW?**

# 10. JUDAISM'S CONTRIBUTIONS TO THE ENGLISH LANGUAGE

*Words and concepts: Kiddush . . . Kaddish . . .*
*Yahrzeit . . . Yizkor . . . Kosher/Kashrut . . . Tallit*
*. . . Tefillin . . . Yarmulke/Kippah . . . Bentschen*
*. . . Bris/Brit/Circumcision . . . Challah . . .*
*Chupah . . . Holy Ark . . . Eternal Light . . . Star*
*of David . . . Siddur . . . Machzor.*

LISTEN TO THE RADIO AND WATCH THE TELEVISION NEWS, and don't be surprised to hear certain words that have become part of the English (or perhaps more correctly American) language. An expert is now a *maven*, unsurpassed gall is *chutzpah*, a *shmir* is a smear (usually of cream cheese, applied to a bagel), a *metziah* is a bargain. There also is a separate genre of not-so-nice words based largely on Germanic or

Slavic terms describing the male organ; these are not heard on the air. Most people assume that these are Yiddish words that have found their way into modern English usage via the large number of Jews who are authors, playwrights, screenwriters, and journalists and who often have found that Yiddish is a superbly expressive language that through translation would lose its special flavor.

For Jews, listening to a character on the screen or on TV use a Yiddish word easily and comfortably (e.g., *shamas* for private detective) is a source of delight and undoubtedly strengthens their sense of rootedness in America.

Since the arrival of Gorbachev on the political scene in the Soviet Union, there is a popular story making the rounds. It seems that President Reagan, who in his earlier years was surrounded by Jews in the movie industry, and who undoubtedly picked up certain Yiddish expressions, was reported to have said during a briefing with the press that he planned to "stop futzing around" and get down to brass tacks on a given issue.

The conversation was reported to the Soviet chairman in detail, of course. The word "futzing" was left intact, since apparently nobody knew how to translate the term. Purportedly Gorbachev turned to an aide and asked, "What does this mean? Futzing?"

The aide did not know, nor did anyone else in the Kremlin, until one academic staff member ventured a guess that it was a Yiddish word. "So?" Gorbachev replied. "Send someone to get a Yiddish dictionary and we'll look it up."

There was a strained silence. Finally one of the aides spoke up, apologetically.

"We can't, Comrade Chairman," he said, his voice quite low. "We burned all the Yiddish dictionaries last week."

The fact of the matter is, however, that there are hundreds of words and terms in Jewish life that are used all through the year, sometimes mainly on the Sabbath or in connection with a particular holiday celebration, that either are unknown or only faintly known to large segments of the Jewish community.

For example, go to the synagogue. Among the more affluent, the synagogue often is called the temple, and among the older generation, the poorer sections of Jewry, or the Orthodox sector, it is generally referred to as the *shul*. How come? This is, after all, a German/Yiddish word meaning a school, a place of learning. The synagogue usually is described as having three principal functions: it is a house of prayer, a house of assembly, and a house of study. The last is the most important function of the three.

Why people attend services in a synagogue is undoubtedly a complex question, but I believe that large numbers of those who go of their own free will (they have neither a special joyous occasion to celebrate nor are they obligated to recite a memorial prayer) do so because they are impelled by a strong desire to learn. A good rabbi with an insightful explanation of a few biblical lines often can fulfill that intellectual need, as can a knowledgeable teacher.

Mastery of the basic words of Jewish life can make it so much easier for anyone wishing to deepen his or her knowledge of Judaism. Start with the home, for example. What is that little box traditionally affixed to the doorpost of a Jewish home (on the right, as you enter, and at a slant)? It's a mezuzah, a container in which a few biblical verses are included, since the Bible instructs Jews to "write them (the words of the *Shema* prayer) on the doorpost of your home." Some Jews will touch the mezuzah lightly upon entering or leaving and kiss their fingers. To some people it may be seen like an amulet; to others it is a symbol of a home whose inhabitants have faith in God.

Once in the house, a visitor may be asked if he would like to join the family for lunch or dinner. If the response is affirmative, then chances are the guest will be handed a small skullcap (*yarmulke* in Yiddish, *kipah* in Hebrew), and after washing he may be honored by being asked to recite the *motzi*. This is the prayer said upon eating bread, which merely thanks God for "bringing forth bread" from the earth (*motzi* means to bring forth).

Of course if it is Sabbath eve or a holiday, then the meal will begin with *kiddush*, the special blessing over wine, whose words are adjusted to be suitable for a particular holiday or for the Sabbath. The word *kiddush* means sanctification, and should not be confused with a word that sounds a little like it: *kaddish*. The *kaddish* is a mourner's prayer, a special and very ancient liturgy that is said by a son for a deceased parent for eleven months after the parent's death. It also is recited for a spouse or next-of-kin. The *kaddish* is in Aramaic, and it is necessary for a minyan—a quorum of at least ten adult males—to be present during the recitation.

After the first year is over, a mourner also is expected to say the *kaddish* prayer five times a year: during the special Yizkor (memorial service) in synagogue on Yom Kippur, Shmini Atzeret (eighth day of Sukkot), Passover, Shavuot, and on the anniversary of the decedent's passing. The last personal memorial usually is called a *yahrzeit*. Many people light special twenty-four-hour *yahrzeit* candles on the eve of Yom Kippur and on the anniversary date of an individual's death.

Among Conservative, Reform and Reconstructionist Jews, more so than among the Orthodox, the requirement to recite *kaddish* for a deceased parent also is undertaken by a daughter. There also are situations where it is impossible for anyone to recite the prayer, and so often a widow or widower, as the case may be, will arrange for an elderly resident of a home for religious retirees to recite the *kaddish*. A gift to the institution, or sometimes to the individual, usually will seal the deal.

For someone not raised in a traditional Jewish setting, the recitation of the *kaddish* prayer (thrice daily at morning, afternoon, and evening services) may seem like a difficult undertaking. The question also may be posed: What for? After all, the decedent cannot hear the words. What's the point?

It's difficult to explain, but the system works if the mourner understands that the prayer he is reciting is for *him*, not for the deceased. The *kaddish*'s ancient words are meant to convey the feeling that the reciter accepts God's decision with respect to the death of his loved one and is abiding by it.

As the days and weeks become months, the person reciting the *kaddish* often finds that he is part of a tiny congregation of mourners within the larger congregation, and that no matter how tragic someone's loss has been, somehow, the daily contact at services, the daily reaching out that takes place in the synagogue, all of it together helps to heal the pain of the loss.

When somebody is told of a person's death, it is traditional to respond with three simple words: *Baruch dayan emet.* Translation: "Blessed is the judge of truth."

If you are invited to a traditional family's home on the eve of Sabbath, you may well be in time to see the mother of the household light the Sabbath candles, often called *bentshen licht,* or blessing of the candles (not to be confused with just plain *bentshen,* which is a term reserved for grace after meals).

Before the lady of the household dons a diaphanous head scarf over her head to kindle the Sabbath eve candles, she likely will take some coins and place them into a charity box, a *pushka*. She will not handle any money after that until the close of the Sabbath—sundown on Saturday. Once or perhaps twice a year she will empty the contents of the *pushka* and forward the money collected to any one of several Jewish charitable groups that are supported in this traditional manner.

Naturally, in a traditional Jewish home there will be *challah* on the table on Friday evening, that light, braided Sabbath bread, which even has a special Sabbath knife to be used when it is cut at the beginning of the meal. Slices of *challah* are handed out to everyone at the table.

On Sabbath eve in a traditional home (as well as on Sabbath at lunchtime), there will be singing between courses. These are liturgical songs, many of them centuries old, with melodies handed down from one generation to another. These songs, thanking God for His bounty, are known as *zemirot*.

Over the years you have heard certain words that you did not understand and had no way of checking. You also have seen certain symbols, religious objects, ritual appurtenances, and you wondered about them. For example, there is the so-called Jewish star, the six-pointed Shield of David. Some people refer to it as the Mogen Dovid, or in more modern Hebrew, Magen David. You have heard that in Israel there is a nationwide organization that uses the Red Magen David as its symbol of emergency rescue service, very much like the Red Cross in America or the Red Crescent in Islamic countries. A small red Shield of David on an Israeli's auto license plate means the driver is a physician. Whence came the symbol? Does it date back to biblical times? Does it have special significance?

Actually, the hexagonal symbol was used both by Jews and Christians in ancient times for decorative and magical purposes. It became a strictly Jewish symbol as of the seventeenth century, and was incorporated into the design of Israel's flag when the Zionist movement formally was launched at the end of the nineteenth century. Some people interpret the two interlocking triangles as symbolizing the physical and spiritual halves of mankind.

Other words that have been heard but not always fully understood include *tallit* (or *tallis*, pronounced the old-fashioned way); and *tefillin, siddur, machzor, shuckeling, shmona esray, mitzvah, gezuntheit*. When someone is sick, he is wished a *refuah shlaymah*. When someone is very ill, his next of kin or friends will go to synagogue and offer a *mi sheh-bayrach* prayer. When someone has a birthday, particularly an older person, well-wishers voice the hope that he/she will live to be 120.

A *tallit* is a prayer shawl worn by men at morning services and in the evening of Yom Kippur. At each of four corners there is a fringe called a *tzitzit*. It usually is white and made of wool, cotton, or silk. An *atarah*, often made with gold thread, is sewn into the part of the *tallit* that lies on the neck and contains the blessing that is recited when the *tallit* first is put on.

It is customary for a Jewish young man to receive a *tallit* at his bar mitzvah from his parents or grandparents. It also is traditional for a bridegroom to receive a new *tallit* from his prospective parents-in-law on the eve of his wedding.

In some synagogues there are nowadays rather innovative forms of the *tallit:* instead of being white with stripes of blue, they run the gamut from dark green to bright red. Some women worshipers also wear a *tallit* at prayer, although not in an Orthodox service.

When a person is honored by being called to the Torah at a Sabbath or holiday service (or on Monday or Thursday mornings, when a brief part of the Torah is read aloud), it is customary for him to take hold of the *tzitzit* of his *tallit,* touch the part of the Torah that is about to be read, kiss the *tzitzit,* and then recite the proper blessing. (At the conclusion of the Torah portion reading, he again kisses the Torah via his *tzitzit* before reciting the closing blessing.)

When a man dies, he normally is buried wearing his *tallit.* The body of the deceased first is washed and cleaned, enclosed in a special garment called *tachrichin* (a white burial shroud), and, if the deceased is a man, his *tallit* is draped around him before the body is placed into the coffin.

Tefillin is the word used to designate the two black boxes that are attached to leather thongs in which biblical excerpts are enclosed. One box is attached to the left arm (unless the worshiper is left-handed, in which case the process is reversed), close to the heart; the other box is placed on the head. When the leather straps are wound around the worshiper's left arm seven times and then tied ritually to the hand, the letter *shin*—representing Shadai, or God—forms on the hand.

A visitor to an early morning service during the week (the

*tefillin* are not used on the Sabbath or holidays) who enters the synagogue and sees a group of men enveloped in prayer shawls with little black boxes sticking up on their heads, and hears them intoning the prayers in a steady singsong rhythm, may at first be startled. If he is sensitive he will observe that each worshiper seems to be in direct, personal contact with God, seeking through prayer to elevate himself just a little higher, spiritually speaking.

Perhaps the visitor should at this point pick up the *siddur*— the prayerbook—and find the first words that are said after the *tefillin* (which are known in the dictionary as phylacteries) are put on: "I will betroth You to me forever; I will betroth You to me in righteousness and justice, in kindness and mercy; I will betroth You to me in faithfulness, and you shall know the Lord."

This passage from the biblical prophet Hosea is recited every morning during the working week. The worshiper is enclosed in his prayer shawl with the *tefillin* affixed to his arm and forehead. One could almost say that this daily morning prayer is like a daily Pledge of Allegiance—to God.

The *machzor* is the special prayerbook for the High Holy Days, the ten days (known also as the Days of Awe) from Rosh Hashanah (New Year) to Yom Kippur (Day of Atonement). *Shuckeling* is a Yiddish term that describes the fervent swaying that some worshipers—usually Orthodox or Hassidic Jews—engage in during a prayer service. The *Shmona Esray,* which means Eighteen (blessings), also is known as the *Amidah,* the standing prayer. This is the silent part of the service where each worshiper communes directly and personally with God. The major part of the daily, Sabbath, or holiday service is offered as a community prayer. During the High Holy Days, for example, when confessional prayers are added, a worshiper who may have led an exemplary, totally ethical life during the year just past nonetheless will join in unison with his fellow worshipers and recite the ancient prayers: "We have sinned, we have transgressed . . . forgive us, pardon us."

A mitzvah is a commandment in Judaism, and almost always also denotes a good deed. A person soliciting funds for an indigent, for example, may clinch his appeal by saying to the prospect, "Come on, throw in ten dollars—it's a mitzvah!"

There cannot be many people in the United States or in the West for that matter, who do not know that the word *gezuntheit* means "to health" and is usually pronounced when someone sneezes. What is not so well-known, however, is the term *refuah shlaymah*, literally "a full recovery," a hope offered to someone ill during the course of a visit or in a written or telephoned message.

For someone who is about to undergo surgery, or who is on a hospital's critical list, a prayer often is offered in the synagogue at a time when the Torah is read. It is called a *mi sheh-bayrach* prayer, and when it is recited a hush usually falls over the congregation so that when the special words are concluded the entire assembly of people can respond "amen" with a little extra fervor. Traditionally, in the case of a desperately ill person, a name is added to his or her name in the hope that it will speed a full recovery. The name that is appended is generally *hayim* (for a man), meaning life.

At a joyous occasion like a birthday party, especially for an older person, the hope often is voiced that the guest of honor reach the age of 120. It's an odd number, until one realizes that it is based on the number of years that Moses lived.

# 11. SYNAGOGUE RITUALS

*Going to synagogue for a bar/bat mitzvah, for an aufruf, for naming a newborn girl, for a special prayer for the sick, for a wedding ceremony . . . How to conduct oneself in synagogue . . . if you're called to the Torah.*

A TIME-WORN HEBREW PROVERB STATES: *lo ha-baishan lomed:* "The shy person does not learn."

When a person is unaccustomed to entering a synagogue, he or she may feel uncomfortable. It may overwhelm such people to hear that they are in a "house of God" and they may be made uneasy by customs or practices that they do not understand.

This is a great pity, for the last thing the synagogue should be is a cold, forbidding, museum-like edifice. A synagogue, if it is to reach into the lives of its members and visitors, should be alive with warmth, feeling, and a sense of closeness with God.

Just as a congregation often is an extension of a family, so the synagogue should be regarded as an extension of the home. Yes, it is God's house, a place for prayer, but it also is a place of joy where families celebrate weddings, bar/bat mitzvahs, births, anniversaries and the joyous festivals and holidays. The synagogue also is a refuge, a place where Jews gravitate in times of trouble to pray for a sick relative, to mourn for a loved one, to recall the memory of a family member or a friend.

There are well over three thousand synagogues in the United States alone, ranging in size from the imposing Temple Emanu-El on New York's Fifth Avenue to a tiny one-room basement synagogue located in a Hassidic section of Brooklyn. One thing that a Jew should feel very sure of is that he is welcome in any synagogue in the world, as is the non-Jewish visitor.

Recently I got to know a young (thirtyish) Jewish engineer. He was born in the U.S., educated at Stanford, and held down a very challenging job. Within a half-hour of what I thought would be a social, superficial conversation, he admitted that he felt within him an "enormous void" because he had not been inside a synagogue since his bar mitzvah (a period of nearly twenty years), and he was convinced that it now was too late for him to reacquaint himself with Jewish practices.

I tried to reassure him that it was never too late.

"The great Rabbi Akiva did not even know how to read till he was forty," I said. "The biblical commentator Onkelos was a convert to Judaism whose insights have been studied by rabbis and scholars over a period of many centuries."

"But I don't even know how to walk into the synagogue anymore," the young engineer complained. "I don't want to be embarrassed by my ignorance."

So, for that engineer and for anyone else who feels a desire to draw closer to Judaism and is not quite sure how to begin, here are some basic rules. They could not, I am convinced, be easier.

You don't have to be a dues-paying member to enter a synagogue or worship there. Every Jew who wishes to take part in a service is welcome, as is every non-Jew who either is interested in witnessing a Jewish service or is invited to participate in a family's *simcha,* or joyous event. If a visitor enters a synagogue that is well-attended, chances are no one will pay attention. If there are only a small number of people present, it is entirely possible that he will be glanced at by some congregants—but not because he is unwelcome.

Sometimes a rabbi or a congregant will approach a visitor and bid him or her welcome. If the visitor is in synagogue to participate in a *simcha,* chances are that he will sit with the other guests. If he is in synagogue entirely on his own, it is possible that someone will ask him whether he is new in the community or whether he has suffered a loss and has come to recite *kaddish.*

The truth is that some people like to slip into a seat quietly and not be annoyed with questions by strangers. There are other people who probably will feel irked that no one came forward to extend a warm welcome to them.

I have worshiped—*davened* is the popular term—in synagogues all over the United States, Israel, and in western Europe. I always have felt welcome and at ease, although some synagogues were warmer and friendlier than others. At a bar mitzvah reception in Jerusalem, the host urged all the people in the synagogue to enjoy the sumptuous foods he had prepared. The same thing happened at a large synagogue in Cincinnati, but in Las Vegas, I was startled by the cool reception of the rabbi and cantor. It later dawned on me that there might be some fears in some circles in that gambling community that a stranger in town, even one who attends services, also might be an undercover investigator for a government agency.

In terms of attire, coming to the synagogue on a Sabbath or holiday is different from attending a service during the week. Daily work clothing is perfectly acceptable during the work week, but on Saturday and on holidays congregants and guests are expected to wear something a little special in keeping with the specialness of the day.

Let us assume for a moment that it is Sabbath morning and you and your wife have been invited to a service and reception in a Conservative synagogue on the occasion of the *aufruf* of a neighbor's son. The *aufruf*, best translated as "call-up," usually is celebrated by a groom on the Saturday morning before his wedding. The call-up refers to his being called to the Torah. In most modern synagogues the bride and groom both are in attendance, and the rabbi will generally offer the young couple a special blessing and extend a gift from the congregation, such as a *mezuzah* to be affixed to the doorpost of their new home.

You both have dressed properly for the occasion, and you even came on time. At the doorway there is a box of *yarmulkes* for the men and a box of lacelike doilies for the married women to cover their heads as well. (Some synagogues even provide bobby pins to keep the head coverings well-fastened.) Now as you gaze inside for a moment, you realize that all the men seem to be wearing a *tallit*. Sure enough, there is a rack filled with prayer shawls, and you take one, drape it around your neck, and remember that a long time ago you used to know the proper blessing to be said when donning the *tallit*.

A special note for Gentile visitors: The *yarmulke* is not regarded as a religious appurtenance, and non-Jewish visitors are expected to wear one, as well as the head covering for married women. However, the *tallit* is regarded as a sacred part of Jewish ritual, and is meant to be worn by Jews only. During the service when the congregation either sits or stands at various times, all people in attendance are expected to follow the congregation's custom. A non-Jew may think he will look out of place if he is the only male not wearing a prayer shawl, but this is not so. The congregation is accustomed to having a few Gentile guests almost every time there is a *simcha*. Since the prayer book and the Bible have

English translations, there is virtually no problem for the non-Jewish guest following the service.

In the overwhelming majority of modern synagogues, the prayer book is carefully divided into sections enabling even the casual reader to follow the service. In addition, the rabbi or whoever is in charge of the service frequently calls out the page numbers and announces where the place is, so that nobody should have a problem of keeping up.

Of course it helps if you can read Hebrew; in most cases the larger part of the service is in Hebrew. If your Hebrew is weak or nonexistent, most of the prayers are translated and can be read in English. In fact, most modern synagogues include a few English prayers—usually a special prayer for the leaders of the United States, for peace, and for the well-being of Israel.

In a busy synagogue you may hear announcements by the rabbi or by the congregational president about newly engaged couples, the birth of members' children or grandchildren, or a special prayer for the recovery of seriously ill people. You may hear the rabbi charge a bar or bat mitzvah, his words meant both for the youngster and for the congregation. Often you may learn that a bar/bat mitzvah celebration is being "twinned" with a particular Jewish child in the Soviet Union who is not allowed to conduct a religious ceremony, with the missing child's name prominently displayed on an empty chair. You also may hear the rabbi bless the new parents of a newborn infant girl who is being named in the synagogue that day. (Newborn infant boys are named at the time of their circumcision ceremonies, usually held at home or sometimes in the hospital where they were born.)

The rabbi very well may deliver a formal sermon, usually one of the high points of a modern synagogue service. In all likelihood he will seek to find a particular passage in the week's biblical reading, and link it to current issues of the day. You might be surprised to learn how certain themes —like greed, brutality, wastefulness, ecology, freedom, and ethical conduct—repeat themselves through the centuries.

At the end of the Sabbath morning service, which usually lasts till around noon, there usually is a collation and informal socializing. If you wish to speak to the rabbi or the cantor or anyone else, do not hesitate to do so. They are quite accustomed to people approaching them with questions and sometimes with rebukes ("you left out so-and-so's name," etc.).

If you were called to the Torah during the Torah reading portion of the service, all you need remember is that the blessings are printed in large letters in English transliteration on a board near the scroll. You take the fringe of your *tallit,* kiss the Torah where indicated, and say the blessing before the reading and again after the reading. Of course, when asked, be prepared to give your Hebrew name and the first name in Hebrew of your father so that you can receive the appropriate blessing. (Some people now add their mother's name too).

There is one time during the year when entry into the synagogue is not always open and simple, and that is during the Rosh Hashanah and Yom Kippur period. Congregation members either receive tickets for admittance as part of their dues or buy the special holiday tickets at members' prices.

Although traditionally the High Holy Days is the one time during the year that the overwhelming majority of Jews wish to step into the synagogue for prayer, for the recitation of the Yizkor memorial, or for the purpose of spending a little time with relatives or friends, it also is the one time during the year that a synagogue has an opportunity to obtain much-needed income to keep the institution going all through the year.

This situation sometimes leads to unpleasant scenes in front of a synagogue building, where uniformed guards often are posted to see that the only people admitted are those with proper tickets. It is true that there are some affluent congregations that dispense with tickets altogether, and anyone and everyone is welcome during the holidays. There also are many synagogues that offer new members drastically reduced dues for the first year of membership as an inducement to future affiliation.

In a perfect world there would be no need for tickets for the holidays; in the real world, where bills and salaries have to be paid, the need exists. Therefore, if you plan to attend High Holy Days services, check first to be sure there is a ticket put aside for you.

In recent years there has been a new facet of synagogue life. Do not be surprised, when you visit a synagogue where you are not known, if you sense that you are being looked over with a degree of suspicion. Since the spread of the cults and the expansion of certain aggressive missionary groups in recent years, it has been learned that some "spies" from the cult or missionary organizations have tried to infiltrate the Jewish community. Most of their efforts are visible at street corners, where they hand out literature amid loud imprecations that the public join up with them. But there also have been reports of some of these people entering synagogues, striking up conversations with young, vulnerable, impressionable members, and trying to win them over.

A non-Jew or a Jew who has had no formal Jewish education may become confused in the synagogue when he picks up a prayer book. In the vast majority of cases, the book reads from right to left as does Hebrew. The book in hand has not been misbound; one gets used to the right-to-left flow in a matter of seconds.

Many synagogues, although by no means all, now feature what are known as egalitarian services—women are honored on a par with men. This is a fairly recent development, and some older, traditional people or younger people unaware of this innovation may at first look askance at a woman being called to the Torah. One quickly adapts to this innovation, too; indeed, you realize that if anything, Judaism is alive and well and more than ready and able to adjust to changing times. In the age of women's lib, why shouldn't women be honored at the Torah? There is no religious regulation against it, only a centuries-old custom that gradually is being supplanted.

Although it is true that Jews attend synagogue services much less regularly than do their Catholic or Protestant countrymen (according to a recent survey of American religious life), there is little doubt that for the overwhelming majority of Jews—religious or secular, affiliated or not—the synagogue remains the heart of the Jewish community. Ask any Jewish man or woman old enough to have lived through the traumatic weeks before the Six Day War in Israel of 1967 or the painful days that followed the Yom Kippur attack on Israel by Egypt and Syria in 1973. There were no announcements, no phone calls, no newspaper ads. In each case Jews knew they were needed to help their co-religionists in Israel. They wished to demonstrate their unity with the Israelis, and so they came to the local synagogues in droves, often without summons, and brought vast amounts of money and pledged whatever else would be needed to help in the time of emergency. For many of those who came to bring monies and to demonstrate their support for their beleagured co-religionists overseas, coming to the synagogue was as natural as a small child running to his mother with a bloody, scraped knee.

You may be invited to attend a wedding and reception in a synagogue, but this will never be on a Sabbath. Therefore, although you are expected to wear a head covering in the synagogue at all times, this does not apply to a married woman, except when she enters the sanctuary where the ceremony will be performed.

There on the *bimah* (platform) you will see a *chupah* (canopy), under which the bride (*kalah*) and groom (*chatan*) will stand. The rabbi will officiate, sometimes aided by a cantor or even a second rabbi. He will read in full or in part the ancient Aramaic words of the marriage agreement (the *ketubah*). The couple will drink wine from the same goblet, a ring will be placed on the bride's finger as the groom recites the ancient words, *Harei at m'kudeshet li b'tabaat zo c'dat moshe v'yisrael:* "You are consecrated unto me with this ring according to the law of Moses and Israel." (Sometimes a double ring ceremony takes place.) The groom then will stomp on a glass, smashing it to symbolize even at this happy moment our memory of the destruction of the Holy Temple in Jerusalem. He then will turn to his wife and they will kiss, while the guests all applaud and wish one another *mazel tov* (congratulations).

The reception that follows probably will be a very fancy repast, with dancing and drinking all jumbled together to help make the wedding as joyous an occasion as possible. If the young couple is lucky, they will recall the ceremony in the synagogue in front of the Torah scrolls, and the words of the rabbi and of the *ketubah* all the years of their lives.

# 12. TAKING PART IN SYNAGOGUE RITUALS

*How to respond to greetings: on Sabbath or holidays
. . . After being called to the Torah . . . If you carry
or raise or bind the Torah . . . if you cannot read
Hebrew, pray in English . . . Reading the Bible and
the commentator's explanation.*

FROM TIME TO TIME I HAVE SEEN A LOOK OF CON-
sternation come over the face of a visitor to the synagogue,
especially on Sabbath morning or on a holiday. This applied
equally to a Gentile guest and a Jew who is lacking basic
Jewish knowledge.

Let us imagine it is Saturday morning and you are crossing
the threshold of a synagogue for the first time. At the entrance
is a stack of *yarmulkes* for the men and a pile of head coverings
for the women. In some synagogues there are prayer books
out in the lobby as well as Bibles; in other synagogues the

prayer books and Bibles are in the back of the sanctuary or in the special shelves in front of each seat. For the men there are rows of prayer shawls (the *tallit*) as you walk in. (The *tallit* is put on at morning services only, except on Yom Kippur, when it is worn all day as well as on the evening preceding.)

One of the synagogue officials, usually a volunteer congregant, may greet you at the door either with a handshake or a friendly nod. He may say to you, *Gut Shabbes* or *Shabbat Shalom* on Friday evening or Saturday morning. On a holiday you may hear him extend a different greeting to you: *Gut Yomtov* or *Chag Sa-mayach*. These are traditional expressions that probably can be heard in synagogues in every continent and every clime.

The Sabbath greeting merely wishes you a good or peaceful Sabbath, while the holiday wish is for a good or happy holiday. How do you respond? If you can, repeat the same words to the greeter; if you cannot, for whatever reason, mumble something, perhaps, "Thank you, the same to you." Not being familiar with this friendly exchange does not disqualify you for anything. Be assured—you will learn the words after a second or third visit.

There is another form of greeting in the synagogue that an occasional visitor may not be familiar with. Suppose you are called to the Torah. In other words, during the reading of the Torah you are honored by being one of those summoned to the Torah reader's side. During one portion of the reading, you kiss the Torah with the fringe of your *tallit*, recite the blessing, and then do the same thing when the reader concludes your section. The *gabbai* nearby asks for your Hebrew name and your father's name, and offers a blessing for you. Then, before he signals to you that you may now return to your seat, he shakes your hand and says, *yashar ko-ach*. As you return to your seat, it seems everyone wishes you the same thing, pumping your hand as though you were running for office. Everyone—the rabbi, the congregation's officers, the cantor, people sitting near the aisle—shakes your hand and repeats *yashar ko-ach.*

The best way to translate the Hebrew phrase is "well done." Your response either can be a simple "thank you" or you can repeat in Hebrew *baruch tihiyeh,* which means "May you be blessed." The same blessings may be extended to you if you are called to open or close the Holy Ark holding the Torah scrolls, or to raise the scroll when the reading is completed (this raising is called *hagbah*), or to roll and bind up the Torah (called *g'lilah*) before the scrolls are returned to the ark.

The good wishes offered to you for having come in close contact with the sacred Torah scroll are sincerely meant. The greeters know that sooner or later they too will be afforded the same privilege of standing alongside the Torah, holding it reverently and knowing that this ancient body of words— written on parchment by hand, one letter at a time—is a blueprint for a positive, peaceful, and happy life for all mankind. It is an awesome privilege to hold or even touch the sacred text. The Torah scroll is Judaism's most sacred object.

If you hold the *siddur* (the prayer book) in hand and realize that you cannot read Hebrew or cannot read it well enough to keep up with the service, do not despair. First, there is the English translation. In the newer prayer books in particular, the translation often is superb. Second, there are various aspects of the service that will not be seriously affected by your lack of Hebrew.

For example, think of the service as being divided between the mind and the heart. In his sermon and in brief comments on the Bible reading of the week, the rabbi will speak in English, explaining, interpreting, commenting, and stimulating you to think about a particular issue or ethical lesson. The cantor, in leading the congregation in the actual prayer, will try to reach your heart by singing ancient melodies, some of which you may know. When the entire congregation joins together in song, it very often is a moving, warming experi-

ence, even if the precise words of a prayer are not fully known
or understood.

Of course, a great deal depends on the synagogue, on the
individual rabbi, on the cantor, and on the overall ambience.
There are some beautiful synagogues that are filled with worshipers who maintain a respectful decorum, and there are
some synagogues where people interrupt the service by constant conversation with neighbors. Among some synagogue-
goers there is a relatively new phenomenon: "synagogue-hop-
ping." Some Jews, anxious to hear the best sermon, the best
rabbi, the best cantor, will attend services at different synagogues, compare notes, and enjoy telling their friends about
a newcomer in the area. This generally does not apply to
Orthodox congregants who attend the nearby synagogue that
they can walk to and from easily on a Sabbath.

What happens if an Orthodox congregant decides he no
longer likes the rabbi or the cantor or the nearby synagogue?
More often than not he and a few other dissidents will start a
new synagogue. Hence, there are many Orthodox synagogues
in the United States, but a great many of them are relatively
low in total memberships.

Thus, going to synagogue services on Sabbath and holidays
can become a combined intellectual-emotional-learning-com-
munity experience. You may very well learn something of
lasting value from the rabbi's talk. You may find yourself, as
you sing, hum, or listen to the cantorial offerings, experienc-
ing a sense of inner peace and relaxation that you had not
known during the work week. There may be something in the
Bible lesson of the week that you never quite realized—some
truth about life, family, humanity, the Jewish people—that
you always took for granted and that you now wished to think
about. You may well enjoy the sense of extended family that
will follow on the communal aspects of the service. Knowing
that you are part of a like-minded group of people who share
your ethical goals and strivings can be a great psychological
lift.

Please do not get the impression that a religious service and the socializing that follow are a somber affair. Quite the contrary. Men and women who see one another regularly at services become friends. They exchange funny stories and share their insights into the news of the day, politics, medical advances, sports, what have you. At the end of a service, two congregants may be heard conversing:

"*Nu,* how'd you like the sermon?"

"Not bad, not bad at all. I think our rabbi's becoming a powerhouse speaker, you know."

"Yeah, I hope he's happy here. Sometimes I'm not sure."

"Well, a lot depends on his wife. He doesn't have an easy job, you know, he's on call all the time—one minute a wedding, and the next a funeral. That's quite an emotional roller coaster to be on, so it's up to the *rebbetzin* (rabbi's wife) to keep him on an even keel."

"By the way, did you notice that the bride this morning is a convert?"

"I wasn't sure. I saw her father alongside, he wasn't wearing a *tallit,* but I wasn't sure."

"Yeah, the groom's parents told me. They're crazy about her, she's a real doll. And her parents don't seem to be too unhappy."

"Well, you never can tell."

If you attend a Sephardic synagogue, you may find a slight variation in the blessings extended to you after being called to a Torah honor. Congregants will wish you *chazak baruch* after your honor, which means "Be strong and blessed."

In a Sephardic synagogue you may also discover that there are certain synagogue melodies that you are not familiar with, since the Sephardic liturgy differs somewhat from the Ashkenazic. In a modern Ashkenazic or Sephardic synagogue, you will find that the cantor will from time to time introduce new melodies into the liturgy. He may use something he picked up during a visit to Israel, or something he wrote himself. Depending on the season of the year, he may even adapt a suitable melody to a particular prayer. At a service, for example, that falls around Israel Independence Day (generally in May), the cantor may adapt the melody of Hatikvah, the Israeli anthem, to one of the concluding hymns.

A special comment is needed here about reading the Bible. Reading is the wrong word—you cannot read the Bible. You have to study it, and at different ages you understand the Bible on different levels. One of the greatest difficulties the Jewish community has nowadays is the study of the Bible. Many children receive some biblical instruction in their early, formative years, in religious school through illustrated children's books and even via videocassettes and films. That's fine as far as it goes, but then, in the overwhelming majority of cases, the child goes forward with his or her education in high school, college, and beyond, but does not study the Bible any longer. There thus develops a vast gap of understanding; for the Bible, to be understood and appreciated and to become a truly lifelong source of guidance and inspiration, must be studied and probed all through life.

In the preface to the first English translation of the Bible that appeared in 1384, the words of the translator resound to this day: "The Bible is for the government of the people, by the people, and for the people." In 1918 English author Israel Zangwill said, "It is precisely in the Old Testament that is reached the highest ethical note ever yet sounded by man."

A taste of biblical study and interpretation can be obtained at a synagogue service, but it is only a taste. The Bible must be studied with as good a teacher as can be obtained, in class, formally or informally. There are small groups of Jews—friends, neighbors, congregants, colleagues—who take time every week or two weeks to sit down with a competent person and probe the meaning of a few lines of the Bible. Such groups are available in synagogues, community centers, through a *havurah*. If there is no such group, organize one!

Quite often a group of intelligent people will come together to study the Bible and will alternate as study leaders. Each person will seek insightful explanations; offer these to a group meeting; and the class will dissect, digest, and discuss the results. Some of these informal study groups have been meeting continuously for years. My own wife leads one such group of women, who meet once a month in one another's home. After ten years they concluded reading and studying the Torah, the Five Books of Moses. It may take another ten or more years for the other two-thirds of the Hebrew Bible.

Heine, who called the Bible the "great medicine chest of humanity," wrote of the Bible in 1840:

"What a book! great and wide as the world, rooted in the abysmal depths of creation and rising aloft into the blue mysteries of heaven. . . . Sunrise and sunset, promise and fulfillment, birth and death, the whole human drama, everything is in this book . . . it is the book of books."

In recent years English-language newspapers of Jewish content, as well as the *Jerusalem Post* overseas weekly, have begun to publish the incisive explanations by talented rabbis of the weekly reading of the Bible. These comments often are very provocative and serve to lead the reader back to the sources.

# 13. JEWISH IDENTITY

*Jews join synagogue (and Jewish organizations) in U.S. to show their identification with Jewish community and to bolster own sense of identity . . . Participating in a circumcision ceremony and in a Pidyon Ha-Ben.*

THE UNITED STATES IS ONE OF VERY FEW COUNTRIES IN THE world where a citizen or visitor can move about freely and legally without having to carry an identity card. In most other countries a policeman can stop anybody and demand to see identification documents. You simply cannot pick yourself up and move from place to place without notifying the local authorities as to who you are, where you came from, how you earn a living, and what you plan to do in a particular area.

In the closing years of the 1900s it seems that more and more people are uncertain about their true, innermost identity. Confusion drives tens of thousands of people to therapists who presumably seek to help these patients sort out their past, their present, and hopefully their future. It is easy to conclude, rightly or wrongly, that ever larger numbers of

117

young people feel unsure about their feelings toward their parents, the opposite sex, their careers, the world as a whole, and life itself.

Every time I read about a teenage suicide, I feel a deep sense of anguish. What an unnecessary tragedy! For what? school grades? a broken romance?

A long time ago, the great sage Hillel, taught; "If I am not for myself, what am I? And if I am only for myself, what am I? And if not now, when?" Hillel lived and taught some two thousand years ago; his provocative words make you wonder: Has human nature changed at all in the last two millennia? Not really, it seems.

First, Hillel advises, think of yourself—your identity, your life, your welfare, your plans. But don't overdo it; don't think only of "numero uno." If you think only of yourself, what are you, really, other than selfish, self-centered, egotistical? Think of your own well-being first, and then share your life, give of yourself, help the next fellow. Finally, don't procrastinate. Putting off the performance of a good deed, for yourself or for another person, imperils the deed's implementation. It may never get done. In other words, don't just float through life, reacting to events and people and situations. Take your life in hand and march forward with a goal and a plan in mind.

What, a reader may ask, does this have to with being Jewish? The answer is—everything.

The sad truth is that there are large numbers of Jews, especially in the larger metropolitan areas of the West, who have lost their way as Jews. In a pluralistic society like America, what's the point of being Jewish? Is it good for your career? Will it make you happier, healthier, richer? Or quite the contrary, will being Jewish limit your opportunities to advance socially or economically?

Sad to say, despite the lessons of the Holocaust, there still are sizable numbers of Jews who wish they had been born

WASPs. For these people Judaism and the Jewish people are an unwanted yoke. For some of these unfortunate people, their inner anger at having been born Jewish and being stuck with the label has led them to become self-hating anti-Semites. Thus, if a Jew in the 1990s harbors no ill will toward Judaism or the Jewish people, but quite the opposite, senses that the Jewish people have over the centuries made enormous contributions to society and have suffered ignominiously at the hands of haters and killers, and if he genuinely wants to affiliate with the Jewish community, then he is to be congratulated and encouraged. He has embarked on the road to discovery of his Jewish identity. Over a period of time, he in all probability will learn more about the Jewish religion and culture and forge his own links with the Jewish community. If he is fortunate he also will find that certain spiritual/psychological/intellectual voids that he was not even aware of are gradually being filled as he begins to lead a Jewish life and expands his understanding of what being Jewish is all about.

A funny thing happens to American visitors when they go to Israel. This applies equally to Jews and Gentiles who come to see the old-new land. They notice that there are thousands of synagogues all over the country, mostly small houses of worship; and yet, when they ask friends, relatives, or tour guides if they, the Israelis, go to services regularly they often get back a peculiar stare of incomprehension.

It turns out that in Israel, where some eighty-five percent of the population is Jewish, the only Jews who attend services regularly are those who are religiously committed. These people account for perhaps twenty percent of the Jewish population. As for the other Jewish Israelis, they explain that just living in Israel, studying the Bible in school for many years, speaking Hebrew, celebrating the Sabbath day of rest on Saturday rather than Sunday, observing the Jewish holidays as national events, hearing a daily biblical phrase broadcast on radio and television in the original Hebrew—all these and more phenomena enable the average Israeli to maintain his Jewish identity with little or no effort. But obviously this is not so in America or in the West. In the United States the Jewish community is only two-and-a-half percent of the total population. To retain one's Jewish identity, no matter how superficially or profoundly, means belonging to a synagogue, to a Jewish organization, to a YM-YWHA, or Jewish community center. It means subscribing to a Jewish newspaper or magazine, contributing regularly to Jewish charities, attending a Jewish lecture or concert. It means, in effect, standing up and being counted.

In May 1967 the Jewish communities of the world jointly underwent a unique, traumatic experience. The news from Israel was ominous: The Egyptian dictator, Gamal Abdel Nasser, had massed hundreds of tanks and tens of thousands of soldiers along the Eyptian-Israeli border in the eastern Sinai region. The Syrians and Jordanians had mobilized in full strength, ready to pounce. Nasser had closed the straits leading to Israel's southernmost port of Eilat, and he had expelled the United Nations forces that had been keeping the peace in the area. President Lyndon Johnson was waffling about sending in American naval vessels to aid the Israelis. Israeli foreign minister Abba Eban was flying from one Western capital to another in a vain effort to persuade somebody, anybody, to try to talk Nasser out of launching an all-out attack. The Egyptian dictator had promised his people that he would drive the Israelis into the sea.

Jews in the United States, Europe, Latin America, and even behind the Iron Curtain where the news trickled through in distorted form feared the worst. In those terrible days of late May 1967, it seemed that a second Holocaust was about to be unleashed against the Jews of Israel. It was a time for Jews to be counted, and they did not falter. Aged pensioners came to the offices of the United Jewish Appeal, bringing their bankbooks and saying in effect, "Take it all. If Israel goes down money will mean nothing to me." Synagogue members and nonmembers alike came together, checks in hand, and offered help. Here and there a Gentile friend proffered a gift, and his gift especially was appreciated. Throughout the world where there were Jews—affiliated or unaffiliated, committed or not committed—there was a sudden, powerful urge to identify with the Jewish people.

It was as if the Jews at the time were saying: If Israel is destroyed in a second Holocaust only twenty-two years after the end of World War II, then we don't want to live in such a rotten world. What good is the money we have? Take it and use it to defend the Jews. Because when all is said and done, I am a Jew, too. I may not be a prophet, but I am descended from prophets.

The Israelis, God bless them, always have been realists par excellence. They succeeded in defeating the Arab attackers in a brilliant, brief, and decisive war. The day was saved. The offices of the UJA and other Jewish institutions where Jews had brought their donations prior to the outbreak of war were kept busy for months, just counting the vast amounts that were contributed and acknowledging their receipt to tens of thousands of donors.

During that crucial time there were some Jews who stood aside and did not have the courage to step forward and rally to Israel's side, but fortunately they were very few in number.

The lesson to be learned from this and from Hillel's teaching is clear. In the Diaspora, where Jews constitute a tiny minority, it is a given that they must affiliate somehow, somewhere, if they truly care about the organized Jewish community. If it strengthens their own sense of Jewish identity and deepens their own understanding of themselves, then that has to be considered a bonus.

One of the fundamental Jewish religious rites is the circumcision ceremony, often referred to as *bris* or *brit* in more modern Hebrew. It is a ceremony during which the newborn infant male child is formally named (his lifelong Hebrew name is given and the biblical commandment—"Every male among you shall be circumcised . . . [as a] sign of the Covenant between Me and you"—is carried out. The citation from Genesis is clear-cut: God says "at the age of eight days every male among you shall be circumcised throughout the generations. . . . This is My Covenant which you shall keep. . . . And the uncircumcised male shall be cut off from his people; he has broken My Covenant."

When a guest arrives at a circumcision ceremony, which usually is held at home, he often is bewildered by what greets him. Everybody seems to be in a festive, happy mood. A table is laden with food and drink for the guests after the ceremony. Most of the men are wearing *yarmulkes;* some are nervous, assuring one another that when the *mohel* (the ritual circumciser) does what he has come to do they will look away.

There on a table is the subject of the guests' oohs and aahs—the happy, relaxed, newborn baby. Nearby the *mohel* is preparing his instruments and equipment. He always is a religious man who in all likelihood has learned his peculiar skill from his father. He likes to amuse his audience with stories about the British royal family, all of whom have been circumcised by a *mohel* rather than a surgeon. (In some small Jewish communities, where no *mohel* is available, a rabbi will officiate at the ceremony and allow a physician to perform the actual rite while he leads the guests in the suitable blessings.)

To a person not raised in a traditional Jewish home, the ceremony might seem outdated, notwithstanding the fact that numerous physicians maintain that it is an important health measure (while some medical people dispute this claim). In Jewish tradition a Jewish son who is circumcised is a full-fledged Jew, a member of the Jewish people and in a very real sense a partner with God in the ancient covenant that was established between God and the Jewish people.

What usually happens at the ceremony is that the *mohel* says a few words to welcome the new child into the Jewish community. After he actually does the circumcision and the infant begins to cry, the *mohel* will dab some sweet wine on the child's lips, which usually ends the wailing. Thereupon everybody will wish one another *mazel tov,* the baby will be taken away to rest, and the guests will be invited to partake of the food and drink provided. Generally, the honor of holding the baby just before he is circumcised is given to the grandfather, who is designated at that point the *sandak* or godfather.

According to Jewish religious law, a Jewish male who is not circumcised still is a Jew, but he is stigmatized as being different. One of the sidelights of the exodus of more than two hundred thousand Soviet Jews from the Soviet Union in recent years is the problem of adult circumcision. Some of those Soviet Jews who settled in Israel or the United States wanted to be circumcised even though they were adults. Many were, but at an adult age the ceremony becomes something of an operation. The word about the surgery and attendant discomfort spread, and subsequently a number of Soviet Jews opted only to have a symbolic circumcision—the drawing of a droplet of blood.

Although circumcision is almost universal among Jews, it also is practiced very widely in the United States, where it often is performed routinely in the hospital soon after a child is born.

In the 1920s some German Jews who were anxious to climb the rungs of society chose not to have their sons circumcised. There were a few cases where such young men were able to save their lives during the Nazi era; their lack of circumcision helped convince their captors that they were not Jews.

There also was a case of an Israeli, a former German Jew who was not circumcised, who was selected by the *Mossad,* Israel's intelligence service, to go abroad, pose as a Gentile, and carry out an espionage operation. He was able to pass as a German Christian until he finally was caught.

Another ceremony that involves a newborn infant son deals

only with the firstborn son. Such a child needs to be "re-deemed," for otherwise (in biblical times) he would have to devote his life to the priesthood and service of God. The ceremony, known as *pidyon ha-ben,* or redemption of the firstborn son, comes into play if the father is not a kohen or levite and the mother is not the daughter of a kohen or levite. If the child was born by Caesarean section the *pidyon ha-ben* rite is omitted.

The ceremony itself takes place a month after the child's birth. The father redeems his child from a kohen, usually a member of the local synagogue, in exchange for five silver dollars (the Torah ruling refers to five shekels of silver). In almost all cases the kohen takes the proffered money and turns it over to charity after the simple ceremony.

Increasing numbers of Jewish couples in recent years have begun to adopt children, either because there is a medical problem in the husband or wife, because a child was orphaned in an accident, or because that is the couple's preference.

There are many questions that have to be settled before an adoption can be fully acceptable according to Jewish law. For example, if the child to be adopted is the product of a Jewish family, or at least if he or she had a Jewish mother, then certain rules apply. But if the child being adopted is not Jewish, then the child must undergo formal conversion. In this case there is one set of rules for a little boy and another for a girl.

The rules of conversion for adults are, if anything, even more complicated than they are for children. Anyone planning to marry a non-Jew who has expressed readiness to convert to Judaism should visit a rabbi and receive a full set of instructions and regulations. There is an old Yiddish refrain, "It's hard to be a Jew." For anyone thinking of converting to Judaism, the refrain applies—perhaps even more so.

But just being Jewish and enjoying Jewish life is sur-prisingly easy if you have the right frame of mind and the right attitude.

After nearly four thousand years of uninterrupted peoplehood and a marvelous record of contributions to humanity, the Jewish people is still here, still laughing, and still working hard to achieve a better world for all. Jews still optimistically look forward to that messianic era when life on earth will be nothing short of Edenic.

So we must be doing something right.

# 14. DEATH, DIVORCE, AND CULTS

*Going to a funeral: the chapel service, interment, visiting the mourners during* shiva *period . . . Another sad moment: a "get," the Jewish divorce . . . Rabbinical counseling . . . Children who get caught up in cults or with missionaries*

JUDAISM CHERISHES LIFE. AT THE SAME TIME THE JEWISH attitude toward death is respectful, even reverential. The psalmist wrote that the "dead cannot praise the Lord . . ." while the Torah was given to the Jewish people so that "you shall live" by its teachings and "not die through them."

The first book of the Bible, Genesis, makes it very clear: "For dust you are and to dust shall you return," and then Ecclesiastes adds: "But the spirit returns to God who gave it." Although by and large most Jews probably do not believe that life in this world is a prelude to "the world to come," such a belief is ingrained in Jewish tradition. The Talmud teaches that "all Israel have a share in the world to come."

The regulations and traditions that have evolved over the centuries vis-à-vis death, funerals, and mourning pragmatically are aimed at offering consolation to the decedent's survivors and to maintaining a sense of dignity and honor for the individual who died.

Through the centuries there has remained a steadfast tradition among virtually all Jews that when the time came for them to be buried they would find their eternal rest in consecrated ground in a Jewish cemetery. Throughout Europe there are many hundreds of centuries-old Jewish cemeteries, large and small, attesting to the importance of this tradition. In northern California, among other locations in the United States, there are a number of small Jewish cemeteries that date back to the gold rush days. Wedged between the financial district and Chinatown in lower Manhattan, there still exists a minuscule Jewish cemetery dating to colonial times.

Perhaps that is why young Jewish families join organizations that offer burial plots. Sometimes members of a large family will buy a lot in a cemetery with room for a score or more people. In outlying communities some synagogues offer burial plots as part of their membership benefits.

There are specific rules and regulations concerning burial. Before a corpse is placed in a coffin, it must be washed and clothed in a simple white shroud. There are groups known as *chevra kadisha* who take it upon themselves to perform the final washing of the corpse: women wash women and men do the same for men. It is considered an honor to be invited to participate in such a group, all of whose members usually are observant Jews.

A male decedent is wrapped in his *tallit*, but not until the fringes of his prayer shawl are invalidated, symbolizing the fact that he no longer is required to perform earthly duties. Embalming and cremation are not permitted in Jewish law. In recent years, however, a number of Reform Jews have been opting for cremation. It also is against Jewish custom to have an open casket at the funeral service, the belief being that it is better to remember the deceased as he or she was in life. Closing the casket is viewed as a sign of respect.

Interment traditionally takes place as soon as possible after death; it may be delayed only to allow close relatives who live a great distance away to arrive in time for the funeral. Funerals do not take place on the Sabbath or on a holiday.

During the time that the body of the deceased is in the funeral home, awaiting the service and final journey to the cemetery, it is customary for a family member or a religious person to sit with the body and read from the Psalms. Such a person is called a *shomer*, a watcher.

If you are planning to attend a Jewish funeral to pay your last respects to the deceased, remember that this is a solemn, mournful event and dress accordingly. *Yarmulkes* are provided for the men. Often there is a memorial page to be signed, indicating to the family that you were in attendance.

Generally, the first row or two of the chapel will be filled with the decedent's closest relatives. Spouses, children, and parents in mourning already will have met with the rabbi who will officiate and will have had part of the clothes they are wearing cut to symbolize the death of a loved one. (Some people affix a black ribbon in lieu of cutting their garments.) There are no special seating arrangements except for the immediate family.

Attendants at Jewish funerals know from experience that if they arrive a half-hour or more earlier than the time designated for the service, they will be able to spend a few minutes with the mourners in an anteroom. These few minutes afford the visitor an opportunity to express personal words of solace to the bereaved.

The actual service is brief. The rabbi will read from the Psalms both in Hebrew and English. He may ask a cantor to join him in a mournful dirge. The rabbi then will speak of the deceased and attempt to console the mourners by urging them to remember the decedent's life of achievement. Throughout the service the casket—covered with a simple spread adorned with a Star of David—rests in front of the room with the deceased inside.

The trip to the cemetery follows the service. At the burial site the casket is lowered into the ground, and those who have come to the cemetery may, if they wish, heave a shovelful of soil onto the coffin to show that they have accepted God's decision to end that individual's life on earth.

In the week following interment, the immediate family customarily observes the *shiva* period. The word literally means "seven," and refers to the seven days when the mourners stay at home, seated on low benches, to remember the deceased.

It is during this *shiva* period that friends come to pay a *shiva* call, a consolation call. Strangely, many mourners in the first week of mourning often appear to be in relatively good spirits despite their loss. The mourners, apparently realizing how difficult it must be for their visitors, try to make the visits as lighthearted as possible. After the *shiva* period is over and the visitors cease to come, what generally happens is that the reality of the loss finally hits home and the mourners feel their loss weeks and months afterwards. It is customary for mourners to recite the *kaddish*, the mourner's prayer, three times daily, especially during *shiva*. Sometimes there will be a *minyan* (ten-man quorum) in the home, and the service will be held right there. At other times the mourners will go to the nearest synagogue to join the regular prayer service. (Some Conservative and Reform Jews will count women for a minyan.)

During *shiva* the male mourners usually do not shave or have a haircut, while the women refrain from using cosmetics. Sexual relations are avoided during the week. Some mourners read certain parts of the Bible: Lamentations, Job, and the sections in Jeremiah that speak of grief. Traditionally, friends or neighbors prepare meals for the mourners during *shiva*. The mourners usually sit all week and wear slippers. It is a custom for all mirrors in the home of mourners to be covered during *shiva*.

When you go to pay a *shiva* call, be aware that in most cases the door of the mourners' home will be unlocked. Walk right in, greet the mourners, sit down, and engage them in conversation to deflect them from thinking of their loss. On the other hand, if the mourners wish to talk about the deceased, then by all means do so as well.

Some people like to bring cake or sweets to a house of mourners. Other people, aware of the fact that the mourners probably have been inundated with these high-calorie items, prefer to make donations to deserving charities in memory of the deceased. Bringing flowers to a mourner is not a Jewish tradition.

After the week's *shiva* period, many people extend the time of mourning for a month; this is known as *shloshim,* which means "thirty." Many men do not shave or cut their hair for the full period of *shloshim*. In synagogue a mourner is not called to the Torah until after the *shloshim* period is past.

It is a custom to erect a monument on the grave of the deceased within the year after the death, usually toward the end of the year. The ceremony of dedicating the tombstone, which generally bears the Hebrew name of the deceased as well as his or her date of death or age at death, is known as an unveiling. It is a relatively recent custom; some people offer refreshments to those in attendance at the unveiling, either at the cemetery or at a restaurant nearby.

A question often asked by people who have never paid a *shiva* call is, What do I say to the mourner? That's difficult to answer; it really depends on the individual situation. Paying a *shiva* call is meant to console someone, so the words must be appropriate to that person and that particular situation. "You should not know any other sorrow" is an expression that often covers many situations. Traditional people, when leaving the home of a mourner, will often declare to the mourner: *Hamakom y'nachem* ("May God comfort you with all the other mourners of Zion and Jerusalem").

Jewish tradition regards a divorce—a *get* in Hebrew—as probably second after death in terms of sorrow and tragedy. Nevertheless, if a couple is incompatible and there is not a true ambience of *shalom bayit* (a tranquil home); if instead there is unending strife and bitterness, Judaism recommends that such a marriage be ended through a formal divorce. Since in all likelihood the couple was married in a religious ceremony "according to the law of Moses and Israel," the divorce also should be a religious ceremony—a *get*.

One of today's major religious problems confronting the Jewish community in America and other Western countries is the growing number of Jewish couples who obtain a civil divorce but neglect to secure a religious divorce. According to Jewish religious law, such people really are not divorced, and if they remarry (and most of these people eventually do) they in effect commit adultery. In addition, any children born to such a couple are classified as *mamzerim*, or bastards. Jewish religious law holds that *mamzerin* only may marry other *mamzerim*.

That is why you will find rabbis and parents pushing hard for divorcing couples to secure a religious divorce in addition to a civil one. The procedure usually is held under the aegis of a rabbinical court known as a *Beit Din;* two witnesses generally are required. If both the man and woman involved cooperate in the proceedings, the entire ceremony lasts for an hour or two, most of the time being devoted to a scribe writing out a formal *get*. If both the man and woman involved agree on their desire to have a divorce, this constitutes ample grounds for the rabbis in the court to grant their wish.

After a divorce is granted, a woman may not remarry for three months. This is done in order to avoid the possibility that if she married immediately after the issuance of the *get*, and became pregnant, there might be a doubt as to the true paternity of the unborn child.

Most rabbis nowadays devote major parts of their time to counseling their congregants. Problems between a husband and wife often are major issues that confront a rabbi. In all likelihood a modern rabbi will have studied pastoral counseling as part of his training, and he will make every effort to reconcile the disputing couple. However, what often happens is that by the time a rabbi is consulted, things have gone beyond repair in a given marriage.

The problems that arise from a divorce are multiplied if there are children involved. When a Jewish couple divorces, there are times when one or sometimes both spouses will remarry and the new marriage partner will be a Gentile. If there are children from the second marriage, as often there are, the original Jewish children will find themselves with half-Jewish siblings. If the mother in the second marriage is not Jewish, then the Orthodox and Conservative wings of Judaism will regard those children as totally non-Jewish. Perhaps that is why there is a poignant Talmudic citation: "When one divorces his first wife, even the Altar sheds tears." Another Talmudic wit wrote: "When a divorced man marries a divorced woman, there are four minds in one bed."

One of the most tragic developments of the post-World-War-II era is the widespread proliferation of religious cults and aggressive missionary organizations. The number of Jewish youths who have been caught up in these movements is extremely high, and the organized Jewish community is finally seeking to prevent these groups from further incursions into the Jewish community.

I am not talking here about Jews who choose to convert to another religion out of religious conviction or because they wish to marry a Gentile and this is the price they have to pay. This is a free country, and people may make their own choices in life.

What does upset the Jewish community is the activist missionary who believes that Jews must convert to Christianity "to save their souls"—whatever that means. The cults run a wide gamut, from Indian gurus to science-fiction writers, and apparently they found a spiritual void in many young people in this country and managed to plug it with all kinds of peculiar "theological" arguments. The simple truth is that the overwhelming majority of these Jewish recruits were almost totally unaware of their Jewish heritage, often came from broken homes, were solicited when they were away from home and lonesome, became involved with these cult groups, and subsequently were brainwashed to a point where it was impossible to reason with them or convince them to leave the cult group.

A young man I know probably is typical. He left New Jersey and took a job in far-off Texas, where he knew nobody. A spotter for one of the cult groups invited him to a meeting, dinner, and a lecture. He was hooked in a matter of weeks. He earned a good salary as an engineer, but soon he was dividing it in half—half for the cult, and half for himself. His boyhood home superficially had been Jewish. Perhaps if he had had a stronger commitment to his faith and a warmer first-hand knowledge of his people, he would have chosen to visit a synagogue when he got to Texas. In a synagogue he certainly would have met new friends as a matter of course.

The story ended happily in this particular case, but only after the parents hired a deprogrammer who sat with the young man in a locked motel room for forty-eight hours, finally persuading him that he had been duped.

There is a strong feeling of antagonism in the Jewish community against both missionaries and cults. Both are seen as enemies of the Jewish people who, after all, are still in shock from the loss of one-third of world Jewry during the Nazi era. The perception now is that these missionaries and cultists want to cut us down even more!

# 15. HOLIDAYS OF THE JEWISH YEAR

*The Jewish year begins in the fall with High Holy Days . . . Sukkot, Simhat Torah celebrations follow on heels of Yom Kippur . . . Hanukkah, Tu B'Shvat (Jewish Arbor Day), Purim, Passover, Israel Independence Day, Shavuot, Tisha B'Av.*

WHAT DO THE JEWISH YEAR AND THE JEWISH CALENDAR really signify?

In the Jewish calendar the corresponding year for 1990 is 5,750, because Jewish tradition counts from the creation of the world. Yet, in the face of overwhelming scientific evidence that the world as we know it really is millions of years old, how can Judaism come along and say creation took place somewhat less than six thousand years ago?

The rabbis of old carefully and painstakingly worked out the details of the Jewish calendar and the entire system of counting the year, based on the moon's movements. They knew that when the first chapter of Genesis speaks of God creating the world in six days and resting on the seventh, these were not exactly the twenty-four-hour days we are familiar with today. They argued, for example, that the sun was not created until the fourth day, and yet even before there was a sun there is reference to "day one" and "day two." In other words, those prehistoric "days" were more like periods of time.

In Jewish life Rosh Hashanah—the new year—begins on the first day of the Hebrew month Tishrei, which usually falls in September (the exact date varies depending on whether *inter alia* it is a leap year). Ten days after Rosh Hashanah is the awesome day of fasting and prayer known as Yom Kippur, the holiest day of the Jewish year. The ten-day period between the two holidays often is referred to as the Days of Awe.

The sounding of the shofar, the ram's horn, is closely associated with Rosh Hashanah. The overwhelming majority of worshipers who take part in Rosh Hashanah services and who rise to hear the rabbi summon the shofar blower to sound the ancient notes of *tekiah, teruah,* and *shevarim* experience an almost mystical passage of time. The *shofar's* sounds are almost eerie. One listens, wondering whether the shofar sounder will succeed in producing the requisite note. Then when the sounds are emitted, there is a momentary connection with all Jews in all places through the ages, from Mount Sinai on, who have been listening to the same memorable sounds.

Listening to the shofar on the Jewish new year is a given. If someone is confined to bed at home or in a hospital because of illness and cannot be in synagogue to hear those ancient notes, arrangements are made in communities for young volunteers, or sometimes the local rabbi, to come to the bedside of a sick person and sound the ram's horn.

You don't need too much imagination to sense how important the sounding of the shofar can be to a sick person confined to a hospital bed, perhaps awaiting a serious operation, on the eve of Rosh Hashanah.

A Jerusalem lawyer, an observant Jew, came to the United

States for serious brain surgery. He told his secretary that he would feel better if he could hear the shofar since it was almost Rosh Hashanah. The secretary, an American girl, phoned her mother in New York and asked if she could make some kind of arrangement for her boss. The mother phoned a friend who in turn phoned a synagogue located about a mile from the hospital, in Manhattan. The synagogue sent a volunteer shofar blower together with a supply of kosher holiday food and wishes for the patient's speedy recovery. The Israeli lawyer heard the ancient ram's horn sound, accepted the good wishes of the area synagogue visitors, had his operation (which was successful), and returned to Jerusalem a healthy person.

You cannot adequately describe the awesomeness that envelops people who are in synagogue on Rosh Hashanah when the shofar blasts are heard. The sounds seem to reach out from eons ago to the depths of a person's soul. The theme of the High Holy Days, in which Jews are urged to repent, pray, and perform good deeds, never is felt more deeply than when the shofar blasts reverberate through the synagogue.

Traditionally, Rosh Hashanah is the time of year when God "writes in" each person's fate for the coming year, and Yom Kippur is the day when He "seals" His decision. During this period God is described in the special High Holy Days prayer book (the *machzor*) as Judge and King. Rosh Hashanah also is known as the Day of Judgment and the Day of Remembrance (for obvious reasons).

There is a strong conviction in Judaism that as much as Jews pray on the holidays for God's forgiveness, it is essential that each person who may have committed a sin against another first obtain that person's pardon. Jewish tradition holds that without the offended party's forgiveness, God will not forgive anybody. People who may or may not have committed any transgressions against anyone during the year just concluded will approach a friend, relative, or neighbor and say in effect: "If I have sinned against you, please forgive me. If I have offended you in any way, please pardon me." It only is after the "offended" party assures the other person that he or she is forgiven that the holiday is approached with hope and a positive attitude.

People greet one another just before the holiday with phrases like *Gut yahr!* (Good year!), *L'shanah tova tikatevu* (may you be inscribed for a good year), and *Gut yomtov* (happy holiday). Holiday greeting cards flood the mail during this period. People wear their best clothes on Rosh Hashanah. The table at home is festive and features a round rather than oblong *challah,* the circle symbolizing a crown for God's kingship. Honey also is on the table to help usher in a sweet year. On the afternoon of the first day of Rosh Hashanah (a two-day holiday), observant Jews generally walk to a nearby river or spring to perform the *tashlich* (casting) ceremony. Pockets are emptied and the contents (lint, usually) are "cast" into the water to symbolize the casting away of our sins. In actuality, *tashlich* often serves as a social event for young people to visit with one another on a holiday, dressed in their finest.

Two other aspects of the holiday should be remembered. On the Saturday night prior to Rosh Hashanah, the synagogue conducts midnight penitential services known as *selichot*. In many synagogues the rabbi will hold a class a few hours before midnight to remind his congregants of the special High Holy Days laws and customs. Another aspect of the pre-holiday observance is the traditional visit to the cemetery in the month prior to the Days of Awe. There is a tradition that the souls of loved ones, who are interred in their final resting places, will intercede with God on behalf of the pre-holiday visitors. It is a popular custom, for it affords people an excuse to visit the graves of loved ones at least once a year.

Yom Kippur, the Day of Atonement, is a day of fasting, prayer, and self-examination. Since all Jewish holidays, as well as the Sabbath, begin on the evening before the day itself, Jews generally sit down to a hearty, pre-fast meal around three or four in the afternoon of Yom Kippur eve. By five-thirty or six, in most communities, worshipers are on their way to the synagogue, cognizant of the fact that they will not eat or drink again until after sundown of the following day.

At home special *yahrzeit* memorial candles are lit in memory of loved ones. These candles will last through the fast and even an hour or two beyond. In synagogue the men all are enveloped in their prayer shawls; white *yarmulkes* dominate. The women also often are wearing white, the color of purity. Very observant Jews may be seen wearing sneakers or other non-leather shoes, leather being considered a symbol of war.

At the appropriate moment the service begins with the ancient, haunting melody of Kol Nidre. The congregation stands during this part of the service. All the scrolls of the Torah have been removed from the ark and are being held by leaders of the congregation. The familiar words and melody resound through the synagogue, and each worshiper is lost in his or her own thoughts: *What lies in store for me next year? and for my family? Will it be a year of peace or a year of strife?* Some, perhaps those who survived the Holocaust, blink back a tear as they recall their traumatic experiences under the Nazis. Other worshipers sense in the melody and words of the Kol Nidre prayer all the tragedies of Jewish history, when so many Jews were massacred for their faith.

On Yom Kippur day itself, the service generally begins at nine in the morning and continues until three or so in the afternoon, when there often is a brief break. Services resume around four and conclude with the sounding of a single blast of the shofar, signaling the end of the fast and the holiday. There is a predictable mad rush home to "break the fast," which often becomes a festive occasion for many people. It is traditional before and on Yom Kippur to wish one another a *gemar chatimah tovah*, best translated as a wish for "a good sealing in" (in the book of life).

Throughout the year there are three daily services: *shacharit*, for the morning; *mincha*, the afternoon service; and *maariv*, the evening service. On Sabbath and holidays there is an additional service known as *musaf*, which means "additional." On Yom Kippur only there still is one extra service, recited only on this day. It is called *ne'ila*, which means "locking in," or conclusion.

Thus when two elderly Jewish friends meet after not having seen one another for a time, and one asks the other, "How're you doing?" the other may respond with a wistful smile and say, "Well, you know, it's almost *ne'ila*."

The book of Jonah is read at the services on Yom Kippur, the only time of the year it is formally read aloud to the congregation. Tradition explains that Jonah was selected because it is the story of a man who tries to flee God and eventually learns that this is impossible because God is everywhere and with everyone always.

Four days after the conclusion of Yom Kippur, the Sukkot holidays begin. The word *sukkot* means "huts," reminding us of the temporary, makeshift huts that the ancient Israelites lived in during the forty-year period when they wandered in the wilderness before entering the Promised Land. Sukkot also is marked as the final harvest of the year.

Walk through an Orthodox section of New York, Los Angeles, Tel Aviv, London or wherever, and you will see these little booths erected almost immediately after Yom Kippur. Traditional Jews eat and sometimes live in the hut for the entire week of the holiday. The purpose of the hut is to emphasize the need to trust in God, as our ancestors did after the Exodus from Egypt, and not put too much stock in material possessions.

It is customary to invite people to share a meal in the *sukkah* (singular of *sukkot*)—a tradition known as *ushpizin* (hospitality) that also is seen as a kind of omen of messianic times. During the holiday itself Jews may be seen blessing a citron (*etrog* in Hebrew) and *lulav* (literally, a palm frond, but actually a combination of a palm, myrtle, and willow). These four are known as the "four species" and are blessed in compliance with a biblical command: "Take the product of goodly trees, branches of palm trees, boughs of leafy trees and willows of the brook and rejoice before the Lord your God seven days."

There is a special way to hold the *etrog* in the left hand and the *lulav* in the right and recite the appropriate blessings. If you visit someone's *sukkah*, chances are that you will be shown how to do so; the same holds true if you go to the synagogue on the Sukkot holiday. You also may see the beautiful procession around the synagogue by all those holding a *lulav* and *etrog*, as well as the moving ceremony as the worshipers pray, *lulav* in hand, and wave their palm fronds in every direction to acknowledge God's presence everywhere. All this while the cantor chants a Hossanah to the Lord.

The eighth day of the Sukkot holiday is known as Shmini Atzeret. Yizkor memorial prayers are recited on this day, and a special prayer for rain also is intoned. The following day, Simchat Torah (the Rejoicing of Torah), marks the conclusion of the annual reading of the Bible, and the beginning of the reading cycle for the new year. In Israel, Shmini Atzeret and Simchat Torah are combined in one day.

If you come to the synagogue on the eve of Simchat Torah, you should not be surprised to see what may at first look like a madcap celebration. The custom is for every male (and women as well in many synagogues today) to carry the Torah scroll around the synagogue in one of seven circumlocutions. The reader, sometimes the rabbi or cantor or a lay member, calls out the names of those who are to hold a Torah, and everybody begins to sing, kiss the Torah, and when the procession around the sanctuary is ended, join in an impromptu dance. Do not be surprised to see that the cantor or the rabbi even is wearing something silly—a strange-looking hat, or a Groucho Marx mask, or whatever. It's all part of the holiday, which essentially calls for rejoicing that we have finished another year of reading and studying the Torah and now are about to begin the yearly cycle all over again.

The person who gets to be called to the Torah for the concluding section of Deuteronomy is known as the *Hattan*

*Torah,* "the groom of the Torah." The person honored by being called to the Torah for the first section of Genesis in the year's new reading is called *Hattan B'reisheet,* "the groom of Genesis."

The next holiday in the Jewish calendar is really a festival; it is not a holy day but a time for festive celebration. This is the well-known Hanukkah, which is celebrated at the same time of year as Christmas. Since Jews wanted their children to have a celebration that had some of the joyous spirit (and the gifts for the children) of Christmas, Hanukkah won out.

Actually, Hanukkah marks the victory of the Maccabees over the Hellenists-Syrians more than two thousand years ago when enemies of the Jews made a concerted effort to destroy their religious heritage. The Holy Temple had been turned into a profane place, and when the Maccabees led their forces against the invaders and recaptured the temple, they found a cruse of consecrated oil that was ample enough to burn for only one day. But a miracle transpired, and the oil lasted eight days. Hence, Hanukkah today is an eight-day festival, during which a candle is kindled every night by a *shamash* candle so that by the last night there are nine candles burning in the special menorah or candelabrum known as a *Hanukkiyah.*

It is customary for Jewish children to receive Hanukkah gifts from parents and grandparents; some people actually give a small gift every day of the eight-day celebration. Traditionally, people eat *latkes* (pancakes) on Hanukkah, a reminder of the oil in the cruse. (Sephardic Jews eat a *sufganiyah,* a jelly donut.) It also is customary to play Hanukkah games, which utilize the four Hebrew letters associated with the festival: *N*es *G*adol *H*ayah *S*ham ("a great miracle occurred there").

In recent years in suburban America, many Jewish families have put electric Hanukkah lights in the window, often in addition to kindling candles that are best kept on a kitchen or dining room table. To drive through the suburbs in the middle of December and see some windows with Hanukkah menorahs and others with Christmas wreaths or Christmas trees showing is an inspiring tribute to pluralistic America. There even are cases where non-observant Jews, aware of the fact that all of their neighbors were displaying either Christmas or Hanukkah motifs, finally broke down and put a menorah in the window. Perhaps they did not want to be known as neuters.

In recent years thousands of people, both professional and amateur, have devoted many hours and much effort to creating new and quite beautiful Hanukkah menorahs. These can be made from clay, metals, wood, and glass and all are perfectly acceptable so long as it is clear that there are eight positions for the eight candles (or oil wicks) and a special place for the *shamash*, the server.

In midwinter, on the fifteenth day of the Hebrew month of *Shevat,* there is a beautiful festival dedicated to trees. It is known as Tu B'Shevat, or the 15th of Shevat, and also as *Rosh Hashanah L'Ilanot* (New Year for Trees). Most people in the Diaspora observe the festival by eating fruits grown in Israel such as carob, figs, dates, and Jaffa oranges. Donations to the Jewish National Fund for new trees in Israel often are made on Tu B'Shevat.

Purim, the Feast of Lots, is the next festival, and is described in detail in the biblical book of Esther. It falls on the fourteenth day of the month of *Adar* (usually around February). In a leap year, when there is an Adar I and an Adar II, Purim is celebrated in Adar II. The festival celebrates the victory of Queen Esther over the wicked Haman, the king's prime minister who cast lots to determine on what day to order the massacre of all Jews in the vast, ancient Persian kingdom. Haman's plan was foiled by Esther and her relative Mordecai (some say he was her uncle, others insist he was a cousin). Instead of killing all the Jews, ostensibly because Mordecai refused to bow to him, Haman and his family all were hanged and the Jews were saved by royal decree.

The book of Esther is known as a megillah (scroll), and on Purim eve it is read aloud in the synagogue, with each child in attendance holding a *grogger*, a noisemaker. At the mention of Haman's name, the *groggers* are spun, and the collective deafening noise successfully drowns out the very name of this ancient enemy of the Jewish people.

On Purim the rabbis ruled that it is permissible, even desirable, to become so joyous, even so tipsy, that one cannot distinguish between the evil Haman and the good Mordecai. In Hassidic areas in both Israel and the United States, it is possible to see some people drinking heavily in order to become so inebriated that they will mistake Haman for Mordecai and vice versa. Most synagogues on Purim eve are loud, noisy, raucous and fun, particularly for the youngsters and their parents. The rabbi or the school principal in charge may, in fact, develop laryngitis for a few days as a result of shouting for order through the evening.

It also is traditional to exchange food gifts on Purim and to give gifts to at least two poor people. Purim balls and costume parties are frequently held, and in Israel there also is the traditional *Adloyada* parade, during which youngsters masquerade in costumes ranging from space explorers to Tarzan. *Hamantaschen,* a triangular dough dumpling usually filled with poppy seed (known as *mohn* in Yiddish), generally is served during this festival season.

A month later, beginning on the fifteenth day of Nissan, comes the beautiful, popular holiday of Passover, also known by many people by its Hebrew name of *Pesach*. It is one of Judaism's major holidays celebrating not only the deliverance of the Israelite slaves from Egyptian bondage but also the beginning of the agricultural year. At Passover, which falls in early spring, the farmers or more correctly the ranchers witness the calving of their cows.

The principal theme of the holiday is freedom and redemption, and at the seder table when the family and guests sit together recounting the exodus story from the Haggadah in a combination service and festive meal replete with symbolism, each person at the table is urged to think of himself as one of the escaping slaves—and therefore not to take his freedom for granted. Among other things the seder effectively serves as an annual reminder for us to be ever vigilant about protecting our hard-won freedoms.

Most people know that Passover is a time to eat matza (unleavened bread), which is a reminder of the fleeing Israelites who had no time to allow their bread to rise and hence had to eat it on the run. There is a biblical injunction not to eat any leaven during Passover and not to own any. Thus, it is necessary to remove all leaven from the home and ascertain that all cooking and eating utensils are free of leaven, or *chametz* as it usually is called.

There are elaborate rules for Passover cleaning and "unleavening." If you wish to know precisely how to go about this, you should consult a rabbi in your community. There are some Orthodox groups that will come into your home before Passover and, using a blowtorch, cleanse your stove and range. Some people will put away all their regular dishes, cutlery, and cooking utensils, use only paper, plastic or glass products, and buy new metal cooking pots and pans. Many people "kosher" their cutlery and dishes and cooking equipment. But here again there are intricate rules on how—and if—it can be done in every case. Many Orthodox and Conservative congregants "sell" their *chametz* (leavened) foods to their rabbi, and he in turn "sells" it all to a Gentile friend or employee. Thus, using this legal fiction, although you actually do have leavened food in the house during the holiday, you don't own it because the rabbi's designee owns it; therefore, everything is okay.

For Israel's kosher army, the government actually "sells" all of its warehouses, granaries, government food supplies, military cooking and eating equipment, and more to a non-Jewish employee until after Passover.

The Haggadah is the center of the Passover celebration. It is read and sung throughout the seder evening (actually two evenings, since outside of Israel Passover usually is celebrated at two seders). The small booklet recounts the Exodus story and instructs all people taking part in the celebration to re-member the purpose of the holiday: to stress freedom, re-member the bitterness of slavery, and enjoy the company of family. There is a rhythm to conducting the service that differs from household to household. Some people skip over the prayers and concentrate on the songs; others focus on the food (which often is very special) and the camaraderie; and others recite every prayer, discuss every nuance of every story re-counted, indicate the seder plate with its symbolic foods, and try to transform the evening into a memorable religious-spiritual-cultural-family-festive affair that will be remembered until the holiday rolls around the next year.

In addition to Passover matza needed for the seder are Passover wine, salt water, bitter herbs, greens, and a special concoction called *haroset* (made of chopped nuts, cinnamon, wine, and minced apple). A cup for Elijah and ample copies of the Haggadah also are needed, as well as *yarmulkes* for the men in attendance. (For instructions on how to conduct a seder and how to prepare all the necessary ingredients, check with your local synagogue or community center. Many institutions offer special classes or "model seders" prior to Passover. If there is no such class, see *The Jewish Catalog* (Volume 1), published by the Jewish Publication Society. It contains a recommended section on putting a seder together.

For people not familiar with the traditional songs of Passover, there are numerous records and cassettes available from Jewish book and record shops. Once learned, these centuries-old melodies and words will become part of your lifelong heritage.

In cities like New York, with its large Jewish population, it is not at all unusual during the week-long Passover period to see people who normally do not take lunch carrying brown paper bags filled with matza, hard-boiled eggs, fruits, and whatever. Less observant people will go to their favorite res-taurants during Passover and order their favorite sandwiches on matza.

For most tourists visiting Israel during Passover, the total absence of bread—leavened food—is a little startling. What often is surprising is how many Gentile tourists take to the matza, first sampled in Israel.

After Passover the next major celebration is Israel Independence Day, an event that at this writing is forty years old. Many synagogues will add a special prayer in the service on this day, and synagogues, organizations, and centers usually will arrange some kind of cultural program focusing on Israel's establishment in 1948.

Seven weeks after Passover, on the sixth and seventh days of Sivan, we celebrate the ancient biblical holiday of Shavuot, generally called "the Feast of Weeks." This beautiful, significant holiday all too often is not observed to the degree it deserves to be. Consider: It commemorates the giving of the Torah to the Jewish people at Sinai, it marks the first harvest (Sukkot celebrates the year's final harvest), and it recalls the ancient biblical and Temple days when Jews brought their first fruits to the Holy Temple in Jerusalem.

Some Orthodox Jews stay up all night on Shavuot eve to study and discuss the Torah. Homes and synagogues usually are decorated with greens and flowers for the holiday. (The Yizkor memorial service is said on the second day of Shavuot.) The special food associated with this holiday is the popular cheese blintz, although some people substitute cheesecake or other dairy products. The explanation for this is that like Israel, the Torah, too, is described as "milk and honey." Another explanation is a little more fanciful: We eat dairy products so as to put aside our shame that our ancestors worshiped the golden calf, which incited Moses to smash the first set of Ten Commandments in disgust.

Many farming communities in Israel celebrate the holiday by staging first-fruits ceremonies in which the children are adorned with garlands of flowers and greens.

There are two sad days marked during the year that do not properly fall under the classification of holidays or festivals.

The ancient Tisha B'Av, the ninth day of the month of Av, generally falls in late July or August and marks the date when both the First and Second Holy Temples were destroyed, the first in 586 B.C.E. and the second in 70 C.E. Special prayers are recited on Tisha B'Av, and many people fast either the whole day or omit at least one or two meals. In some synagogues worshipers will place candles on the floor, overturn benches, and recite prayers while seated on the floor. Men are not permitted to wear their customary *tallit* or *tefillin* on Tisha B'Av. The special service includes mournful dirges and the reading of the biblical book of Lamentations.

A more recent day of profound sorrow commemorates the Holocaust, during which the Nazis massacred six million Jews, including an estimated one-and-a-half million children. This is known as Yom HaShoah, the Day of the Holocaust, and falls on the twenty-seventh day of *Nissan*. Memorial meetings are held in many places by many groups. In Israel theaters and movie houses are closed for the day.

A kind of half-holiday celebrated mostly by children and youths is called Lag B'Omer (the thirty-third day of counting the Omer), marking the end of a plague that killed Rabbi Akiva's students in ancient times. Many couples marry on this day. Orthodox families often give their sons their first haircut on Lag B'Omer.

# 16. JEWISH REGULATIONS AND PERSPECTIVES

*Keeping kosher . . . Are these regulations really important? Are they dated? . . . What are the Jewish views on women's lib, homosexuality, autopsies, abortion, animals, birth control, hereafter, ecology, slander, nudism, reincarnation, sex?*

OLIVER WENDELL HOLMES WROTE THAT "LIFE IS PAINTING A picture, not doing a sum." The Jewish way of life also cannot be compressed into precise parameters. We cannot cite chapter and verse in Judaism that promises X if you do Y. Judaism is a way of living. It stresses ethical behavior, compassion, and justice both on a personal plane and as a worldwide goal.

Reading and absorbing this volume, or ten volumes, or even a whole library of books still only is comparable to an artist's initial dabbings. There still is so much more to be added to the painting!

If someone were to spend an entire lifetime studying the Jewish sources—Bible, Talmud, the commentaries, the liturgy, history, language, and more—perhaps then he would begin to understand what being Jewish means.

In modern times many people, Christian and Jew alike, assail the "religious" man who prays regularly but who is an evil, unethical person. Some of these critics go further, dismissing prayer, religious services, and even religion itself as hypocrisy or some atavistic vestige of ancient times. They view religion as something totally unsuitable for our own day and age—as if they had discovered something new!

A long time ago the psalmist condemned the thief who offers prayers; his prayers are equated to blasphemy. The prophet Isaiah railed against pilgrims who came to the Holy Temple but whose lifestyles were inimical to Judaism. He proclaimed: "Do not continue to bring Me false offerings and incense, they are an abomination to Me!"

The expression *chillul haShem* can best be translated as meaning desecration of God's name. In Jewish tradition, if a Jew anywhere is found guilty of a crime, Jews feel shame. If that individual was a professing Jew and prayed regularly, then his crime is viewed as a desecration of God's name. Such a person casts shame and anguish on the entire Jewish community.

The discussion to this point introduces a subject that many people do not fully understand and many even disparage. I am referring to *kashrut,* the system of kosher food, one of the tenets of Judaism that unites Jews throughout the world and that has remained a unifying force through their long history.

The word "kosher" has become part of the American language. It really means "fit," and generally is regarded by most Jews as a component of the Jewish way of life. Remember, Jewish law seeks to help make the Jewish people a holy people. Maintaining a kosher home and eating only permitted foods at all times are seen as parts of that overall goal. In Exodus God said, "You shall be to Me a kingdom of priests and a holy nation."

There also is a tradition in Judaism that explains certain laws as being unfathomable, but because they are biblical and handed down by God, we have to obey them and keep faith that one day we will understand the reasons behind these regulations.

Many people today seek to rationalize their observance of the laws of *kashrut* by asserting that these are in actuality ancient health measures. There is no such claim in the Bible or in Jewish teaching, although the net result may be that Jews who abstain from eating pork products, for example, are not subject to diseases such as trichinosis. The removal of all blood from poultry and other meat before consumption, a prerequisite of the kosher food laws, also is seen by many as a disease prevention step. However, Judaism ordains that eating kosher food is required for the purpose of sanctifying the Jewish people. In other words, it is one step on the ladder of Jewishness; it is a form of self-discipline and an act that helps the Jewish people maintain their distinctive way of life.

In Jewish tradition the table is seen as a small version of the altar at the Holy Temple at which sacrifices were made to God in ancient times. Thus, the table and everything placed on it must be holy. As is well known, there are special blessings to be recited before eating and drinking. There also are rules about reciting grace after a meal. If it is true that we are what we eat, then Judaism—which wants us to be as good and holy as possible—feels duty-bound to guide our food intake.

The rules are relatively simple, but problems often arise and should be checked out with a rabbi. For example, if a glass of milk standing in the refrigerator spills onto a closed pot of cooked chicken, is the chicken kosher or should it be discarded? According to the Jewish dietary laws, the only animals that may be eaten are those with cloven hoofs and that chew the cud. Both characteristics must be present. As for fish, only those that have both fins and scales may be eaten. In the poultry category chicken, turkeys, geese, ducks, and doves are permissible. Other fowl may not be permissible probably because they are predatory (hawks, ravens, owls, and the like). Also prohibited are amphibians and insects as well as creatures that crawl "upon the belly," "winged swarming things," and rodents and lizards.

Products such as milk, oil, or eggs that emanate from non-kosher sources are forbidden; the only exception specifically permitted is honey from bees.

The expression "ritual slaughter" has come to be associated with meat and fowl prepared according to the Jewish dietary laws. The Hebrew word for kosher slaughter of animals is *shechitah*. There are many rules and regulations surrounding slaughter, all of them meant to assure the purity of the animal and that the actual killing of the animal be carried out in as painless and humane a way as possible. The ritual slaughterer is called a *shochet,* and although it obviously is a difficult job—imagine spending your days slaughtering animals!—the Jewish community traditionally always expected the *shochet* to remain a religious, gentle person who would regard his vocation as providing kosher sustenance for the Jewish community.

In the best of all possible worlds, Jewish tradition holds that a vegetarian diet is best for all people. Many Jews agree and regard the *kashrut* laws as a compromise between the ideal and people's baser instincts to consume meat.

One of the basic laws in the Jewish diet prohibits the mixing of meat and dairy dishes. They may not be mixed and eaten together. It is necessary for someone who has eaten a meat or fowl meal to wait, usually six hours, before consuming dairy products. There are very observant Jews who will not eat out except in restaurants that are strictly kosher. There also are observant Jews who compromise: they will eat out in non-kosher establishments, confining their meals to (kosher) fish, dairy dishes, vegetable salads, and the like.

To obtain a better understanding of the Jewish people and decide whether one wishes to identify more closely and actively with the Jewish community, it will be helpful to seek out Judaism's view on a wide range of contemporary subjects. What follows is a brief overview of Judaism's views on a variety of topics.

*Women's Lib:* Jewish tradition believes that if a woman wishes to devote herself to a career rather than home and marriage, that's all right; it is up to her. A woman may be a rabbi, for example, because a rabbi primarily is a teacher. Under ancient Jewish law there have been some areas in which women have suffered discrimination. An example would be divorce proceedings, where the husband generally is put in a better bargaining position. In the biblical story of daughters whose father died, Moses ruled that they could inherit their father's estate just like men. This is seen as an early biblical precedent. In Judaism there always has been a feeling that women should be given an extra push upward to correct the legal inequalities that still exist in Jewish law. Today there are women's prayer groups in which the worshipers put on a *tallit* and *tefillin* and read the Torah. Many Conservative and Reform synagogues afford equal treatment to men and women in honors associated with synagogue worship. For every man who points to a Talmudic dictum that "women are unstable" and "do not take kindly to guests," another will come forward with other Talmudic comments such as: "Women have greater powers of discernment than men" and "a man should love his wife as much as himself and respect her more than himself."

*Homosexuality:* The Bible clearly describes male homosexuality as an "abomination." Indeed, if men should "lie with man, as with woman, they have committed an abomination, they shall surely be put to death." Many rabbis forbid two men from sleeping in the same bed or even sharing a room. (The biblical rulings against homosexuality extend also to non-Jews, under the seven laws of Noah.) Lesbianism also is condemned in Jewish teaching, but not as severely as male homosexuality. Maimonides ruled that a married woman found to be engaging in such practices was not forbidden to her husband, but urged the husband to prevent his wife from associating with women who follow this lifestyle. Interestingly, the commentators and rabbis of old referred to homosexual practices, and not men or women who had homosexual tendencies.

*Autopsies:* Judaism regards the human body as a holy vessel. Tampering with a corpse is considered an act of *nivul ha-met,* desecration of the dead. In Israel today, where the Orthodox rabbinate is the chief source of religious rules and regulations, there is a serious problem about autopsies. Many traditional Jews reject the idea of an autopsy for themselves and their loved ones. They maintain this stance despite the fact that most rabbis have permitted an autopsy where the study of the deceased will benefit other people. Some rabbis even go so far as to insist that all autopsies sooner or later will benefit people. The use of corpses for dissection and study purposes generally is opposed by most rabbis. On the other hand, the transplantation of an organ from a dead person to someone suffering from a disease or handicap now is largely acceptable. The saving of life is a paramount principle. As one rabbi put it: "It is permissible to use a pig's heart to save a dying person because the pig is forbidden as food, but not as a saver of life."

*Abortion:* Centuries ago, the rabbis ruled that it is not permissible to murder one person in order to save the life of another. When the "greater part [of the child] has emerged [from the womb], it may not be touched," they ruled. On the other hand, according to the rabbinical decisions, if a woman finds it very difficult to give birth and there appears to be a danger to her life, the fetus may be cut up while it still is in her womb and removed from the mother. The life of the mother takes priority in such a case. The fetus is not considered a person before entering the world, and may therefore be destroyed to save the mother's life. The rabbis emphasized, however, that once the "greater part" of the infant emerged, it now was regarded as a person and could not be harmed. Most rabbis today permit abortion if they are convinced that giving birth at term would endanger the mother's health or sanity or if they are reasonably certain the child would be born deformed or imbecilic. Other rabbis permit an abortion if the woman was raped, especially if she was married at the time of impregnation. Most rabbis do not permit abortions for economic reasons or merely because the child is not wanted.

*Animals:* Not many people know that there is a strong tradition in Judaism stipulating that animals are to be treated with kindness. Cruelty to animals (known as *tsa'ar baalei chayim*) is strongly prohibited. The Talmud teaches that before he sits down to a meal, a man first should feed his animals. He should care for the animals in his custody. The ritual slaughter of an animal for food purposes must be done with a special knife free of any nick, and the act itself must be done expeditiously and without pause in order to minimize the animal's pain. Jews have expressed abhorrence for the custom of force-feeding geese and of plucking their feathers while they are alive. Vivisection for the purpose of advancing medical knowledge is regarded positively in Judaism, but slaughtering animals for their skin and furs is seen as cruel and offends the teachings of Judaism.

*Birth control:* Judaism teaches that we are to "be fruitful and multiply." The rabbis also cautioned that Jews were not permitted to "waste seed," which most people interpret to mean as emitting semen with no purpose. In ancient times the question arose as to how many children would constitute fulfillment of the commandment about being fruitful. Shamai said two sons would suffice, while Hillel taught that a son and a daughter would be ample. Most Jews in the Western world practice modern birth control methods. Modern Orthodox Jews, who generally have larger families, plan the size of their families, while the more rigidly ultra-Orthodox often do not. In Talmudic times there already was a primitive birth control device in use, known as a *mokh,* a kind of absorbent contraceptive. There is uncertainty today as to whether this was used prior to intercourse or was inserted after the sex act.

*Hereafter:* There is no clear-cut Jewish teaching about the hereafter. The overwhelming majority of Jews probably believe in the doctrine of the "immortality of the soul"—a belief that in the messianic era the soul will reunite with the body and there will be a resurrection of the dead. Rabbinical literature speaks of the "world to come," but this is interpreted differently by various groups. For example, Maimonides understood the phrase to refer only to the soul's immortality. Nahmanides, a great Middle Ages sage, believed in a genuine resurrection. Reform Judaism has formally expressed its view against bodily resurrection, as well as against the ideas of heaven and hell as everlasting abodes for reward and punishment. Judaism is seen by most Jews as a religion of this world; as for the other world, a Talmudic scholar (Rabbi Jacob) in the second century wrote: "Better one hour of repentance and good deeds in this world than the whole life of the world to come; yet better is one hour of bliss of spirit in the world to come than the whole life of this world."

*Ecology:* This is a very new issue that was virtually unknown in previous centuries. There is, however, a lovely parable concerning God and Adam that is applicable. The story says that God took Adam to the Garden of Eden and showed him around. Then He said: "See how lovely and worthy of praise are My works. They all have been created for your sake. Take care not to spoil or destroy My world."

Back in rabbinic times there already were certain proscribed practices that have an ecological echo today. Pieces of broken glass were not to be left in the field but had to be buried deep in the earth. Other rubbish could be buried on public property but only during the winter (when the heavy rains turned everything into a morass of mud). Tanneries, graves, and carcasses had to be separated from the city. Tanneries, whose foul odors were well-known even in biblical days, had to be constructed in such a way that the winds did not waft their smells toward the city. Goats and sheep could not be raised in cultivated areas. Judaism espouses the precept of "do not destroy." Thus, Maimonides taught that "it is not only forbidden to destroy fruit-bearing trees, but whoever breaks vessels, tears clothes, demolishes a building, stops up a fountain or wastes food in a destructive way, offends against the law of 'thou shalt not destroy.'"

*Slander:* Slander is sharply condemned in Jewish life. Jeremiah and the psalmist spoke out strongly against this evil. If a man slanders his wife, casting doubts on her chastity, he is liable to punishment. Written and verbal slander are regarded as equal sins in Jewish life. It is a sharply repudiated transgression, for the sinner/slanderer, for the person slandered, and for the one hearing the slanderous tale—all three are tainted.

*Nudism:* One of the fundamental principles of Judaism is modesty, or *tseni-ut* in Hebrew. Religious teachers seek to teach their students about the importance of dressing unprovocatively. All wings of Judaism regard nudism as an aberration and contrary to all Jewish ideals of behavior. Stripping clothes from the human body and walking around in the nude is seen in Jewish teaching as an affront to man's dignity.

*Reincarnation:* No Jewish religious thinkers, past or present, have ever taken the idea of reincarnation seriously. The mystics associated with the Kabbalah movement expressed faith in the transmigration of souls. There are some Hassidic groups today that also express belief in reincarnation. The famous play about the *dibbuk*—the alleged guilty soul that entered the body of a human being and had to be exorcised— was never accepted by the majority of Jews as an authentic Jewish concept.

*Sex:* Celibacy is totally frowned upon in Jewish thinking. All the great figures of the Bible and the post-biblical period married, had children, and appeared to enjoy normal family sexual relations despite active lives as leaders and teachers. Isaac, Abraham's son, is described in Genesis as "sporting" with his wife Rebecca. The Talmud even declares that a man may not withhold conjugal rights from his wife; indeed, these are part of the marriage contract. The Talmud adds that a woman can expect her husband to be with her "every day" if he is not working. It adds that laborers should grant their wives conjugal rights twice a week. A sailor, on the other hand, need only perform once in six months, presumably because he frequently is away from home.

# 17. JEWISH HISTORY

*Brief history of the Jewish people . . . Abraham, the first Jew . . . Slavery in Egypt, the Exodus, Giving of the Torah . . . When judges ruled, time of kings, northern kingdom cut off, the first Temple destroyed, return to Jerusalem . . . until now.*

A CONCISE OVERVIEW OF JEWISH HISTORY FROM ANCIENT times up to our own day might be helpful here. There always has been a special relationship between Jews and time. The concept of Sabbath is a strictly Jewish innovation. The holidays; the seasons of the year; the special blessings for the arrival of the new month; and even the division of the day into three parts, each of which has a special time for prayer, all indicate Judaism's obsession with time. Is it because our sages deep down understood that every moment of every day is precious and should be used fully, effectively, enjoyably, and usefully? Perhaps. Or is it because we need constantly to be reminded to pause, look around, enjoy God's bounty, and delight in the world that we inhabit and never take it for granted?

Although the Jewish people is very ancient, one of the most inexplicable aspects of Jewish life is the contemporary applicability of the Bible. When anyone studies the Torah, whether it is for the first time or for the umpteenth time, and meets Abraham, Isaac, Jacob, the matriarchs, Moses, David, Isaiah, and others, there is the strongest possible sense of identification with those biblical figures. They seem to step right out of the Bible to live and thrive among us today. Their lives are examples and role models; their teachings are every bit as relevant as when they first were offered; the love and reverence that we attach to them seems every bit as current as when first experienced by our ancestors.

Some Jews believe that when God gave the Jewish people the Torah at Sinai, every Jew in the world, those already born and those not yet born, were there at least spiritually. That may help to explain a sense of déjà vu that many Jews experience when they refresh their knowledge of Jewish history.

The patriarchs and matriarchs lived between the twentieth and seventeenth centuries, B.C.E. (Before Common Era). The Hebrews were slaves in Egypt from the seventeenth to the thirteenth century, when the Exodus took place. Some time between approximately 1200–1020, judges ruled Canaan, which had been conquered in the thirteenth century. King Saul, Israel's first king, ruled from 1020–1004. Until 928 there was a united kingdom (Judea and Israel) under David and Solomon. The kingdom of Judah continued till 586, when the Holy Temple was destroyed and the Jews were taken captive by the Babylonians. Israel, the Northern Kingdom, was overrun by Assyrians and its people deported and scattered in 720.

In 538, thanks to Cyrus, Jews were allowed to return to Judea. In this same century the Torah (Pentateuch) was canonized. By 515 the Second Temple had been rebuilt in Jerusalem. In the fourth century the books of the Prophets in the Hebrew Bible were canonized. In 332 Alexander the Great conquered Judea. Seventy scholars living in Egypt translated the Torah into Greek in the middle of the third century. The Jews, led by the Maccabees, revolted in the second century against foreign (Seleucid) rule and rededicated the Holy Temple (which had been desecrated) in 164. For the next eleven years the country was run by the Jews. In 63 Judea was captured by the Romans and became another Roman province. From 37 B.C.E. to 4 C.E., Herod ruled the country. In the year 30 C.E. Jesus was crucified. In this first century of the new era, there were anti-Jewish riots in Alexandria followed by a massacre in the year 66. In the same year the Jews began their revolt against Rome, and in 70 the Holy Temple was destroyed by the Romans. Three years later the defenders of Masada were crushed, and the Dispersion of the Jews began. Persecutions against Jews took place in the first and second centuries. Canonization of the Bible's third section, known as *Ketuvim* (Hagiographa), took place in the second century.

In 210 the mishna section of the Talmud was edited and preserved. In 219 a great academy was established at Sura in Babylonia. Forty years later another great learning institution was set up in Pumbedita, also in Babylonia. Some time in the fourth century, the Jewish calendar was made a permanent, fixed instrument of Jewish life. In the fifth century the Babylonian Talmud was completed; at the same time, persecutions against Jews began in Babylonia. Jewish rule under the Persians was established in Jerusalem for a few years in the seventh century. Between 624–628 Mohammed led an attack against Jewish tribes of Arabia, destroying most of them. In 638 the Arabs seized Jerusalem.

In the ninth century the traditional Jewish prayer book was compiled. In the next century Jews living in Moslem Spain began a great cultural renaissance. When Spain turned Christian, the Jews' "golden age" began there. In the eleventh century Jews began to settle in England. In the same century the great scholar Rashi wrote his Bible and Talmud commentaries in France. In 1096 Crusaders en route to the Holy Land massacred Jews living in the Rhineland; three years later they captured Jerusalem. In England, in 1144 the first blood libel was leveled at Jews. Across the then-known world, in Egypt, Maimonides wrote his classic works and commentaries. In 1187 Saladin captured Jerusalem from the Crusaders. In 1210 three hundred rabbis settled en masse in the Holy Land. In Paris in 1242, the Talmud was burned on orders of the church. Across the sea Jews were expelled from England in 1290, and in 1322 they were expelled from France. Massacres of Jews took place in the fourteenth century in Germany.

Jews especially were singled out for killing during the Black Death period in Europe from 1348–1350. There were massacres in Spain in 1391, and another expulsion from France in 1394. The Austrians expelled them in 1421. In 1492 Spain expelled the Jews, and the Ottoman Empire welcomed them to its Moslem lands. Portugal in 1496 expelled the Jews and forced others to undergo mass conversion. The Venetians established the first ghetto in 1516; in the same year the Turks seized Palestine. The first printed volumes of the Talmud were completed in 1523 (Hebrew printing began in 1475). A period of pseudo-messiahs ensued. Talmudic volumes were burned in Italy; Pope Paul IV ordered Jews to be confined to ghettos. Jewish settlements in the Baltic and Poland areas grew in the sixteenth and seventeenth centuries. Notorious massacres occurred in Poland in 1648–1659, led by Chmielnicki.

In 1654 the first Jews arrived in New Amsterdam in the New World. Two years later the Jews were readmitted to England. The Hassidic movement evolved in eastern Europe, leading to bitter disputes among Jews. In 1789 the U.S. Constitution gave Jews full equality. Two years later, France's national assembly followed the U.S. example. Russia established a restrictive "pale of settlement" area for the Jews. In 1818 in Hamburg, Jews set up the first Reform temple. In 1837 there was a terrible earthquake in Safed and Tiberias, near the Sea of Galilee. Two years later, in Persia, the entire Jewish community of the city of Meshed was forcibly converted to Islam. In Damascus the Jewish community was accused of killing children for their blood. In Palestine in 1870, a school to train Jews to work the land was set up at Mikve Israel. In the same year Italy's Jews were extended equal rights. In 1878 the first Jewish colony, called Petah Tikva, was founded in Palestine. During 1881 and 1882 pogroms erupted through Russia, and scores of thousands of Jews fled to the United States and western Europe. In 1882 the first organized Zionist group (Bilu) left Russia for Palestine to reclaim the ancient homeland. In New York in 1886, the Jewish Theological Seminary was established. In 1894 Alfred Dreyfus, a French officer, was found guilty of treason; he was later exonerated and freed, but his trial helped Theodor Herzl decide to launch the political Zionist movement. The first world Zionist Congress took place in 1897 in Basel. In Russia in 1903, a notorious pogrom took place in Kishinev, resulting in mass Jewish emigration. During the First World War, in 1915, Palestinian Jews formed a separate military unit and fought alongside the British. In America in 1916, Louis Brandeis was named the first Jewish Supreme Court justice. In 1917 Britain issued the Balfour Declaration, promising the Jewish people a homeland in Palestine. Despite the overthrow of the hated Czarist regime in Russia, vicious anti-Semitic riots broke out in the Ukraine, forcing thousands to flee to the United States, Palestine and Argentina.

In 1921 Arabs rioted against the Jews in Jaffa. In 1925 the Hebrew University opened in Jerusalem. Hitler published *Mein Kampf* in Germany, and in New York Jews organized Yeshiva College, later to become Yeshiva University. Many Jews were killed in Arab riots in Hebron in 1929. The Nazis came to power in 1933 and set up the first concentration camp in the same year. The anti-Jewish Nuremberg racial laws were promulgated in 1935; Arab riots against Jews intensified in the next year. In 1938 widespread attacks on synagogues,

Jewish institutions, and Jewish-owned businesses took place in November and came to be known as *kristallnacht*. It was the beginning of the end of central European Jewry. The Nazis set up ghettos in 1940, and the first death camp (in Chelmno) a year later. The Jews in the Warsaw Ghetto launched a revolt against their oppressors in 1943; in 1944, serious efforts were launched to save the Jews who had not fallen into the Nazis' hands. When the war ended and it became known that six million Jews had been massacred, the survivors—then called displaced persons—demanded the right to settle in Palestine despite a British ban on further immigration. Thousands of Jews reached Palestine between 1945 and 1948 in clandestine journeys. After Israel's establishment in May 1948, large waves of displaced persons from Europe and Jews from Moslem countries poured into Israel.

In 1947 the Dead Sea Scrolls were discovered in a cave overlooking the Dead Sea. In 1948 the Soviets executed numerous Jewish intellectuals and suppressed all forms of Jewish culture. Israel in the same year fought off seven invading Arab armies, signed a ceasefire with most of them, and arranged for the immediate transfer to Israel of 50,000 Jews from Yemen and 123,000 Jews from Iraq. In 1952 Germany signed a reparations agreement with Israel. Two years later, a mass immigration of Jews from North Africa arrived in Israel. In 1960 Adolf Eichmann, the notorious Nazi responsible for the massacre of European Jewry, was captured in Argentina and brought to Israel where he was tried, convicted, and hanged. The Six Day War in 1967 was seen by many Jews as a virtual miracle, since the weeks preceding it terrified many Jews into believing a second Holocaust was in the offing. In 1970 Soviet Jews who had been practically incommunicado with Jews in any other part of the world began to protest for the right to emigrate to Israel and the West, and in 1971 they began to leave the Soviet Union. Although Egypt (and Syria) attacked Israel in 1973 on Yom Kippur, President Sadat signed a peace treaty with Prime Minister Begin in Washington five years later. In 1982 Israel invaded Lebanon in order to crush PLO terrorist forces. In 1987 Arabs living in the West Bank and Gaza Strip, occupied by Israel since 1967, began an uprising against the Israelis.

In 1851 the Jewish scholar and philosopher Nachman Krochmal said that "the strength of Judaism consists in this, that as soon as one period of history comes to an end, another begins. A new idea replaces the old, fresh sources come into play, and the result is continuous progress."

A few years ago the American Jewish community was asked to put together sixty million dollars within a few days to help rescue thousands of Ethiopian Jews who had fled their ancient homes to find refuge in the Sudan and who were in grave danger of being lost to famine and massacre. The funds were raised almost overnight, the money dispatched, and the rescue operation carried out. Today thousands of black Ethiopian Jews can be seen all through Israel, moving swiftly along into the twentieth century, closing the historical gap that had separated them from the mainstream Jewish community for over two thousand years.

Without a perspective of Jewish history, without a sense that all Jews are one through time and throughout the world, it is doubtful that such a humanitarian rescue could have been carried out. In the Jewish community there is a sense of pride in the history of Judaism and the Jewish people. There is pride and also a feeling that the best is yet to come, that in the generations ahead the Jews still will be making major contributions to society.

Many Jews in the free world also have an ambivalent feeling about religious practice. There are, of course, many Jews who pray at services easily and readily. The Hebrew or the English words voice their own innermost sentiments. These are the lucky ones, for in truth there are many other Jews, both "religious" and "secular," who find it difficult to pray. They ask themselves, or a rabbi perhaps, Why is it necessary to keep offering paeans of praise to God? Does God really need our compliments? Does lauding Him make us better people? more ethical Jews?

Yet a large majority of these Jews continue to come to the synagogue through the year for the holidays and memorial services, for they sense that perhaps the more they attend services, the more they pray, the more they immerse themselves into a Jewish spiritual environment, the better are their chances of finding satisfactory answers to their questions.

Perhaps they remember a true story from the Second World War, and the "lesson" of the story speaks directly to them.

During the war there was a time when southern France was not occupied by the Germans. In one particular synagogue in a southern city, Jews who had fled from the north and who lived in that city gathered on a Friday evening for a traditional Sabbath service. The congregants, the service, and the synagogue all were low-key; everyone knew that Jews throughout Europe were in terrible danger and that vast numbers already had been killed deliberately.

There is a part of the Sabbath eve service when the congregation turns around together (to welcome the Sabbath bride), faces the rear, sings together for a few moments, and then resumes their normal position. On that particular evening a band of French fascists, some four or five people, had plans for that congregation. They arrived silently in the synagogue, entered stealthily, and took up positions in the back of the sanctuary with their weapons aimed at the back of the congregation. They awaited only a signal from their chief to open fire.

Then suddenly, without warning, the Jews all turned around, prayer books in hand. The fifty or so Jews stared at the four or five French fascists, face-to-face, eye-to-eye. The Jews must have been aghast to see guns aimed at them. The French fascists, miraculously, could not pull their triggers. They all stood frozen in time. Then the Frenchmen withdrew, unable to carry out their planned attack.

How does one explain that? Was it a miracle? a coincidence?

To look at the problem from an entirely different perspective: Can a Jew be Jewish "culturally" and not have any direct link to the synagogue or religion of the Jewish people? I believe the answer is yes, without question, but being Jewish becomes so much more enjoyable and meaningful when the Jewish religion and culture and history all are united naturally and comfortably.

There are Jews, for example, whose sole link to Judaism's community and heritage is a genuine affection for the Yiddish language. They love its sounds, rich descriptions, wit, and profound insight into people's deepest core. A Yiddish song will bring a tear; Yiddish words that have been adapted as part of the American language fill them with pride; a Yiddish play or musical performance can become a deeply moving, heart-satisfying experience.

I, too, love Yiddish. It is an absolutely delightful language, but so for that matter is Hebrew. And I am sure Ladino—the "Yiddish" of many Sephardic Jews (based on Spanish)—also is a very expressive method of communication. But language and literature simply are not enough to fill the psychological/spiritual voids that confront so many people in this advanced technological age.

It is difficult enough for a Jew who was not raised in a traditional home to learn the mores and practices of Judaism and how to be Jewish. Opting to exclude the religious dimension in favor of only the cultural one is like handicapping oneself before one even gets started.

To enter into the Jewish community wholly and fully, a person has to open his or her heart and mind, receive the heritage that was so many years in the making, assess it, and learn it. Then one should take from it what is truly, personally meaningful.

# 18. THE RELATIONSHIP BETWEEN THE LAND AND THE COMMUNITY

*Israel and the Jewish people . . . special relationship that always existed between the Holy Land and Jewish community . . . "Dual loyalty" an empty phrase . . . Special ambience for Jews in Israel . . . "Next year in Jerusalem" proclaimed twice yearly.*

TWICE A YEAR, AT THE CONCLUSION OF THE HIGH HOLY DAY services on Yom Kippur and at the end of the *seder* service on Passover, it is customary for Jews all over the world to proclaim a centuries-old phrase, *L'shana haba-a b'yerushalayim,* literally, "Next year in Jerusalem."

There are some who are fearful of the phrase—fearful that

non-Jews will accuse the Jews of dual loyalty. They believe that loyalty to the United States is weakened by loyalty to Israel. Of course, this is utterly nonsensical. It is an apprehension that exists only in the minds of insecure Jews who are basically uncomfortable in their Jewishness and who are always, it seems, looking over their shoulder to see what "they" are saying about "them."

First, today it is legal and absolutely possible to be both a citizen of the United States and of Israel simultaneously. There already are thousands of people who enjoy this special privilege. Second, the comedian Alan King put it very well when he was asked on a British television talk show why he was so interested in and supportive of Israel. With a chuckle, he replied immediately, "Simple—I think of America as my wife, as the wife I love and am devoted to, and I think of Israel as my mother. So how can there be a conflict?"

The fact is that in some two thousand years of dispersion, the Jewish people never forgot their ancient homeland for one moment. Prayers for the welfare of the ancient land of Israel are found in the prayer book, with special additions for special seasons (rain for the winter months, dew for the summer period). A great many of the holidays are oriented to the land of Israel: Jewish Arbor Day (Tu B'Shevat), Passover (first paschal sacrifice), Lag B'Omer, Shavuot (first harvest), Tisha B'av, Sukkot (final harvest).

The thrust of the ancient prayers always was in the direction of Zion: "Renew our days as of old." Through the centuries of the exile and dispersion, Jews continued to dream of a return to their ancient homeland where peace would prevail and where each man could sit under his "grapevine and under his fig tree" in security and tranquility.

Among most Jews in the world, no matter where they live, there is a mystical attachment to Israel. After all, the Bible clearly and unequivocally states that God said to Abraham, the first Jew: "Unto thy seed will I give this land."

Isaac Kook, the late chief rabbi of Israel, said "only in the

Holy Land can the spirit of our people develop and become a light for the world." The very air of the country, the Talmud teaches, "makes one wise." One scholar taught that "residence in Israel is equivalent to the observance of all the biblical precepts."

Over and above this mystical, sentimental, emotional link to a land that first nurtured the Jewish people there is a special attachment to the country that especially is meaningful for Jews past the age of fifty.

Those over fifty still remember vividly the black years of the 1930s and the 1940s. There not only was a terrible economic depression that affected virtually everybody in the early and middle 1930s, but there also was a frightening arousal of anti-Semitism in the United States, England, and France, and in other countries. This was stimulated by the rise of Nazi Germany, which proclaimed itself at war with Jews and Judaism. The Jews of the period had no Israel to turn to for physical help or psychological support. The Jewish community in that time to a large extent was deeply depressed, pessimistic, and fearful.

As news of the fate of the Jews swept up in the Nazis' invasions throughout Europe during World War II reached America, there was no place to turn. The Western democracies paid lip service to the plight of the Jews but did nothing to help. In fact, there were cases where some officials of western countries deliberately sabotaged any efforts to rescue Jews endangered by Nazism.

So today Jews throughout the world look at Israel and say to themselves: If there had been an Israel back in the 1930s and 1940s, there might very well not have been a Holocaust at all. Hence, if there ever is any trouble for Jews anywhere in the future, there is an Israel to which they can go freely and openly, thank God.

There is this fundamental bond between Israel and Jews worldwide that binds them. When Jews in the United States hear about some way-out neo-Nazi organization in the West or South that wants to isolate the Jews, and worse, they may say to themselves, "Well, these are only crackpots and don't mean a thing." Or they might say to themselves, "What would happen if there ever is a bad economic time in this country, and the Jews become scapegoats again, as always in history? What would I do? Thank God for Israel!"

In the beginning of this century, an American Jew named Leo Frank was lynched by an Atlanta mob that insisted that he had killed a young Christian girl. For decades Jews protested Frank's innocence but were not able to prove it. A few years ago an old survivor of that period came forward; he had been an eyewitness, he identified the killer and totally exonerated Frank. Reluctantly, the state of Georgia finally issued a posthumous pardon for Leo Frank. But it was grudging; even at this late date, the unjustified murder of a single Jew did not really seem to prick the conscience of Georgia's leaders.

It is with this attitude that Jews approach Israel. They intend to ensure that Israel remains strong, secure, and a haven for those who need her or wish to settle there. This fierce devotion to Israel does not diminish by one iota the loyalty of American Jews to the security and well-being of the U.S.

# 19. A CLOSER LOOK AT JEWISH RITUALS

*A closer look: The functions of rabbi, cantor, sexton, gabbai, Torah reader, Shofar sounder, teacher . . . Breastplate and "rimonim" on Torah . . . Kissing the Torah or a fallen prayer book. Build a sukkah, bake challah, learn Hebrew, enjoy being Jewish!*

FROM TIME TO TIME I AM STARTLED WHEN YOUNG AMERican Jews—quite often highly educated and very intelligent ones—pose questions that seem to me so transparently simple!

One young woman who has been actively pursuing a number of courses in Judaism asked me, "When you recite the *amidah* (the silent prayer), when do you bow your head? Some people, when they recite the *kaddish*, the mourner's prayer, seem to take a few steps back at the end. Why?" In the amidah, the silent prayer that affords the worshiper at services the feeling that he or she is in direct, personal communion with God, it is customary to bend the knees and bow the head slightly after the words *Baruch Atah* (Blessed are You). This is done at the beginning and just before the repetition prayer, known as the *kedushah*. When saying the *kaddish* one feels in the presence of God. Therefore, when leaving we symbolically back out a little, as though we were leaving a royal presence.

Then there are people who ask, "What does a rabbi do? a cantor? a *shamash*? How hard is it to learn Hebrew? After all, it's written backward, from right to left."

Of course, the big questions always seem to crop up. "Pray? I don't know if I can. What does it mean to pray to God? What about the Holocaust? How can I pray to God in the aftermath of that catastrophe?"

Most people, Jews and non-Jews alike, do not know the origin of the Hebrew word *l'hitpalel,* which means "to pray." The best translation is "to judge oneself." When you sit in synagogue surrounded by other worshipers and listen to the cantor lead the service or a rabbi comment on the week's biblical reading, or you hear a bar mitzvah youth chant his assigned portion, you are in a real sense checking yourself out for the immediate past and perhaps the immediate future.

As the pages of the prayer book are turned, as the familiar chants echo through the synagogue, as you see familiar faces, you may (or you may not) recite the prayers. But somewhere in your mind you are asking yourself whether you behaved well in recent days, and you also are wondering about your future relationships with all the people in your life.

Many people are not aware of the fact that they "pray" all through their lives, although not necessarily in a formal service. How often do we say "Thank God" during the day on hearing that someone we care about is well and not ill? Is this not also a form of prayer? When you step into a hospital and look at the faces of the visitors, their very expressions look like prayers for the recovery of their loved ones.

It has been said that in this day and age there are many people, Jews as well as Gentiles, who waver between belief in God and nonbelief and therefore vacillate about prayer. At certain points in their lives, these people are ready to pray—to offer thanks at a joyous occasion, or at the other end of the spectrum, to plead with the Almighty for help and guidance in a time of crisis. There are people who maintain that when you step out into the verdant countryside and enjoy the view of a stream and mountain, that, too, is a form of prayer, for you are in a sense praising God for His bounty.

The pendulum of faith and faithlessness swings back and forth. Not very long ago, around the time of the Great Depression, many Jews turned away from the synagogue, from Judaism, and certainly from prayer. There was so much suffering in the world and so much despair that many could not continue with the ancient prayers and the centuries-old customs and ceremonies.

Then came the Second World War, the Holocaust, and the establishment of Israel. Quite suddenly there was a strong reversal on the part of many Jews—this religious community that was singled out for mass murder would not perish! Indeed, many felt that if we are Jews, then let us be Jewish: knowledgeable, observant, learned. A movement sprang up that has attracted thousands of young Jews in the United States, Israel, and the free world. It is the *Baal T'shuva* movement, best translated as "the movement of penitents." It probably should be called something else, but the name has stuck.

It is not as though those who join this group are former "sinners" who now are repenting. In the overwhelming majority of cases, those who opt to become rigidly Orthodox, as most of the *Baal T'shuva* people do, come from backgrounds that were totally lacking in Jewish content and who found in Jewish observance a way of life that was meaningful and fulfilling.

I think of a friend whose son is a *Baal T'shuva*. The young man, a musician raised in the affluent Westchester suburbs of New York, got involved with drugs. He and his wife were addicted, and who knows where they might have wound up if not for the fact that they somehow were introduced to a charismatic young rabbi who showed them a different way.

Today the young couple strictly observes all aspects of Judaism. They live in Jerusalem where he earns a livelihood as a musician, although now he plays traditional Jewish music instead of rock. He has grown an impressive beard, and a *yarmulke* never leaves his head, while his wife keeps her kerchief on her head at all times. They seem very happy, and the world of drugs must by now appear to have been only a bad dream. For them and others like them, the *Baal T'shuvah* movement has been a godsend.

But what about others? What of American Jews who are not involved with drugs and who have had some Jewish religious training but still find it difficult to pick up a prayer book at a synagogue service and pray? I can only urge these people to make a greater effort, bearing in mind that the prayers that were included many centuries ago in the *siddur*, the Jewish prayer book, were chosen very carefully. They had to express mankind's eternal doubts and hopes; they had to reflect man's unchanging nature. A little study will show even the casual worshiper that they do. Bear in mind that Jewish prayers are divided into four classifications: prayers of petition and supplication, prayers of thanksgiving, prayers in praise of God, and prayers that are essentially self-searching.

The next time you enter a synagogue, pick up a prayer book, and if you wish to join in with the congregational prayers and singing then by all means do so. But you may not be receptive. You may feel like an outsider, a nonparticipant watching a spectacle. In that case, open the *siddur* at random, read a few lines in Hebrew and/or English. You may wish to see the origin of the prayer, when it first was composed, and by whom (the more modern prayer book will have a list of sources). Now perhaps a phrase, a line, a thought from the prayer will touch you.

If someone has been raised in a nontraditional Jewish home, learning how to pray and how to participate fully in religious services is not the easiest thing in the world. But it can be done and is being done almost every day. Indeed, quite a few Orthodox, Conservative, Reconstructionist, Reform, and even Hassidic rabbis came from backgrounds that were totally secular. One of the great rabbis of this generation, a Jerusalem scholar by the name of Adin Steinsalz, was reared in an anti-religious home in pre-Israel Palestine. He was a brilliant student, and everyone predicted great things from him in math or physics—until he amazed his friends and family and chose to become an Orthodox Jewish scholar.

One of the most charismatic young rabbis who has influenced countless young men and women to choose a religious way of life, Shlomo Riskin, emigrated to Israel from the Manhattan-based Lincoln Center Synagogue that he led. He came from a home where the only religious observance he saw was that of his grandmother.

We return to the original question of how to be Jewish. The answers to the question can vary. One person will insist that you practice "hands-on Judaism"—bake your own *challah* loaves for the Sabbath, crochet a *yarmulke,* research your family's genealogy, raise funds for your synagogue or for Hadassah or the United Jewish Appeal or any other worthwhile cause.

Another will insist that you pray regularly; observe the rules and regulations about kosher food, the holidays, and festivals; study the Bible regularly (preferably with a good teacher); improve your Hebrew; read Jewish publications, visit Israel and Jewish places of interest; read Jewish books, listen to Jewish music; and fill your home with Jewish art.

The third person will respond that you should first and foremost *zei a mentsh,* be a genuine, real person—someone filled with kindness and compassion who practices justice for all.

In a way all of the above are right answers. Some people will follow one pattern of life for years, changing and adding or cutting back at certain times. Others will pick and choose, and do only those things that appeal to them.

I think of a friend who had had a thorough Jewish upbring-ing but because of his occupation (there were few fellow Jews working in construction) had gradually drifted away from the organized Jewish community. When I saw him in synagogue, I knew something was wrong. He explained that he had come because his son was about to have serious heart surgery. He wanted to recite a *mi sheh-barach*, a prayer for his recovery. The boy's surgery was successful, and now the father has become a regular worshiper.

There's another worshiper I observe who also now is a regular. His religious background was shallow and his mem-bership in the synagogue an act of identification until about two years ago, when he suffered the loss of a parent and found that the daily service with fellow mourners and worshipers eased his pain and comforted him. By osmosis, I muse, he is absorbing the spirit of the Jewish heritage.

Then there are the mixed couples in the synagogue: Young families where one parent has not converted but has agreed to raise the children in the Jewish faith of the spouse. (Converts to Judaism very often become active leaders of the con-gregation and of Jewish organizations.) But here is a young man, for example, who sits in synagogue with his son, teach-ing him, setting an example for him, and guiding him, but knowing that his wife, the mother of the child, is at home, totally separated from this aspect of her family's life.

No matter how much love and understanding there may be between spouses in such a situation, sooner or later there is bound to be some friction. A child reared "half and half" is put into an impossible situation. The confusion of early years may well give way later to choices that neither Jewish nor Christian parents want. Of course, there always are excep-tions. A youngster raised in a home that is half-Jewish and half-Christian can turn out perfectly well-adjusted, happy, and even boastful about his dual cultural-religious background.

But unfortunately, this often places a heavy burden on a child and on his parents, adding to the risks of normal daily life of the family.

Answers to some of the simple questions posed earlier will follow below:

A *rabbi* essentially is a teacher, someone especially qualified to answer religious questions. In most instances today a rabbi also is a family counselor, a person licensed to officiate at a wedding, a synagogue leader who bestows blessings on a bar/bat mitzvah or a newly wed couple or new parents, and who is called on to comfort a bereaved person and officiate at a funeral.

A *cantor* leads the congregation in the singing and praying at services and therefore touches the worshiper's heart, while the rabbi seeks to impart understanding and wisdom to the worshiper's mind through a sermon.

A *shamash* is a sexton. He makes sure that the prayer books are in place, and often teaches youngsters their bar/bat mitzvah portions (this can also be done by a rabbi, a cantor, a teacher, or a parent).

A *gabbai* is an usher in the synagogue. When the Torah is read aloud on Sabbath and on the holidays (as well as briefly at Monday and Thursday morning services and on Saturday afternoon) he stands alongside the reader to ascertain that the Torah is being read accurately.

A Torah reader usually is called a *baal koreh*. He must know thoroughly the section he is reading since the scroll of the Torah contains no punctuation and no vowels.

The person who sounds the *shofar* on Rosh Hashanah and at the very end of Yom Kippur is called a *baal t'kiyah*. It takes practice to master this ancient skill.

A teacher in a modern synagogue religious school generally has graduated from a seminary for religious teachers. A teacher in a *yeshiva*, an all-day school, usually has a more extensive educational background. The teachers in nursery schools attached to synagogues often are trained in their field but take special courses to learn the Jewish content of their school's curriculum.

The *breastplate* on the Torah, often bedecked with precious stones, reminds the modern congregant of the breastplate worn by the High Priest when he officiated at the Holy Temple in Jerusalem.

The *crown* atop the Torah, placed there when the scroll is carried through the synagogue, expresses the Jewish people's reverence for the "noblest crown of all"—that of the Torah.

The handles that the scroll of the Torah is affixed to are called the *Aitz Chayim*, the tree of life.

The bell-like adornments atop the *Aitz Chayim* rollers, placed there during the Torah procession, are called *rimonim*, Hebrew for pomegranates, which they resemble.

The *Ner Tamid*, or Eternal Light, is the perpetual lamp that usually is found immediately above the ark that contains the Torah scrolls. The eternal light is a reminder of the light that burned continuously in the Holy Temple.

Most synagogues (in the Western world) face east toward Jerusalem. The word in Hebrew for east is *mizrach*, and those who usually sit at the eastern wall (a special honor), are the rabbi, cantor, congregation president, and special guests.

When the Torah is carried through the congregation, many people reach over and kiss it with their fingertips or prayer book or with the fringes of the prayer shawl. (In Sephardic synagogues, most congregants merely throw a kiss toward the Torah.)

If a prayer book falls to the floor, a congregant usually will kiss it as a sign of respect.

If, heaven forbid, a scroll of the Torah should fall to the floor, there are some people who believe it is necessary to fast for forty days. It almost never happens, and probably if it did, a rabbi would be able to find extenuating circumstances to vitiate a forty-day fast.

Many young families living in the suburbs of metropolitan areas have become do-it-yourself-ers. Jewish families have discovered that doing it yourself can add a special dimension to being Jewish. Young couples putting up the traditional, symbolic *sukkah*, or booth, for the Sukkot festival, find it rewarding. Other people have become adept at creating Hanukkah *menorahs* and creative *mezuzahs* to put up on their doorposts (you still have to buy the special parchment enclosure). Daring mothers have brought back the traditional Sabbath dishes of their grandparents' time, like the *cholent* that can be kept warm all through the Sabbath on a low flame (lit before the onset of Sabbath). Those people endowed with artistic talent find a great measure of joy in capturing on canvas the portrait of a parent or grandparent that will hang prominently at home, attesting to the Jewishness of the preceding generations.

Being Jewish can be, should be, and very often is a source of deep enjoyment. It is not a burden; if anything, it is a challenge. Being Jewish means constantly striving to do better ethically, vis-à-vis your friends and family, and with respect to your community and the world as a whole.

The American people have been brought up to enjoy "life, liberty, and the pursuit of happiness." These certainly are noble ideals, but Judaism has a slightly different approach. It teaches that you cannot "pursue" happiness, but if you do certain things and act in a certain way, you will be happy.

Judaism, citing the line in Proverbs, says that those who support the "tree of life" or the Torah are happy. The psalmist taught that those who trust in God are happy. He who does not sin is happy, and the person who does not associate with sinners also is happy. Those who dwell in God's house and fear God are happy, the psalmist says. People who practice justice and show they care about the poor are happy, the psalmist writes, adding that so is the man who earns his living by honest work. Isaiah adds that he who keeps the Sabbath is happy.

The performance of good deeds and a life of the highest ethical standards is the essence of being Jewish. Following this course will bring happiness in its wake. Of course, you also must always continue to expand your learning and knowledge.

I and my wife were lucky. We both were raised in traditional Jewish homes filled with warmth, love, kindness, caring, and joy.

Our respective grandfathers were poor but very happy and serene men. You look at their photographs, and there is a twinkle of pure, unadulterated happiness that comes through. Certainly they never had more than a few nickels at a time to rub together, but they always seemed to be happy. Those grandfathers of yesteryear knew something. They knew what was important and what was not.

For a brief period I turned away from Judaism and from God. I was in my early twenties, and the first reports of the Holocaust had begun to surface. My heart bled for the six million victims of evil and insanity. I grew angry with God for allowing such a horror to take place. I stayed away from the synagogue in that period; my only link to the Jewish people was the work I did, trying to help the survivors of the Holocaust start their lives anew in America and in Israel.

Then a tiny miracle took place. My oldest child, my daughter, was born. What a joy! What a miracle!

I realized quickly how arrogant I was. How did I dare turn away from God and Judaism in the face of the miracle of a new life? I returned to the synagogue and we gave our daughter her Hebrew name (in memory of her great-grandmothers).

Over the years I have asked numerous rabbis, scholars, and thinkers for their explanation of the Holocaust from a Jewish point of view. It turns out that there is no satisfactory answer, so far. Perhaps there will be one in the long-awaited messianic age.

For now, being Jewish every day and in every way is a very satisfying, fulfilling, and enjoyable way of life. If you're Jewish, try it, you'll like it. If you're not—well, just take my word for it!

# FREQUENTLY RECITED BLESSINGS

**Blessing for wine:**
*Baruch atah Adonai Eloheinu melech ha-olam, Borei pri ha-gafen.*
(Blessed are You, O Lord, our God, king of the universe, who creates the fruit of the vine.)


**Blessing for bread:**
*Baruch atah Adonai Eloheinu melech ha-olam, Ha-motzi lechem min haaretz.*
(Blessed are You, O Lord, our God, king of the universe, who brings forth bread from the earth.)


**Blessing for Sabbath eve candles:**
*Baruch atah Adonai, Eloheinu melech ha-olam, asher kidshanu b'meetzvotav v'tzeevanu l'hadlik ner shel Shabbat.*
(Blessed are You, O Lord, our God, king of the universe, who has sanctified us with His commandments and commanded us to light the candle for Sabbath.)

# SUGGESTED READING LIST FOR FURTHER STUDY

Leo Baeck, *The Essence of Judaism*

Milton Steinberg, *Basic Judaism*

Robert Gordis, *Judaism for the Modern Age*

Herman Wouk, *This Is My God*

Cecil Roth, *A Short History of the Jewish People*

Howard Sachar, *The Course of Modern Jewish History*

Abraham J. Heschel, *A Passion for Truth*

Samuel Caplan and Harold Ribalow, *The Great Jewish Books*

Milton Konvitz, *Judaism and the American Idea*

Hayyim Schauss, *The Lifetime of a Jew*

Arthur Hertzberg, *The Zionist Idea*

Abba Hillel Silver, *Where Judaism Differed*

Trude Weiss-Rosmarin, *Judaism and Christianity: The Differences*

Lewis Browne, *The Wisdom of Israel*

Arthur Morse, *While Six Million Died*

Paul Johnson, *History of the Jews*

David C. Gross, *1001 Questions and Answers About Judaism*

David C. Gross, *The Jewish People's Almanac.*

Connor Cruise O'Brien, *The Siege.*

# GLOSSARY OF POPULAR YIDDISH AND HEBREW TERMS

NOTE: Y means Yiddish. *H* means Hebrew. The *ch* is usually pronounced in the hard, guttural way (as in the German *ach*).

| | |
|---|---|
| *Aggadah* | Homiletic parts of Talmud, as opposed to legal sections. |
| *Agunah* | A woman who is in limbo because her husband's whereabouts are not known. |
| *Aliyah* | The honor of being called to the Torah; also used to mean a Jew's decision to settle in Israel. |
| *Am ha-Aretz* | A boor or ignoramus. |
| *Apikoros* | A Jew who negates all Jewish belief. |
| *Ashkenazi* | A Jew whose family came from central or eastern Europe; most American Jews are Ashkenazim. |
| *Aufruf* (Y) | The ceremony whereby a groom is called to the Torah on the Sabbath before his wedding. |

| | |
|---|---|
| *Averah* | A sin. |
| *Baal Agalah* | A simple, coarse person (literally, "a wagon driver"). |
| *Baal Tefilah* | A man who leads congregational service, either during week or in lesser portions of Sabbath/holiday service. |
| *Baleboss* (Y) | The person in charge. |
| *Baruch ha-Ba* (H) | Welcome! (Said to a man; for a woman: *B'rucha ha-ba'a.*) |
| *Baruch Ha-Shem* | Thank God! (A religious person, asked how he is, will often respond, *Baruch HaShem.*) |
| *Beit Din* (H) | A court or tribunal. |
| *Beit Knesset* | A synagogue. |
| *Beit Midrash* | House of study, generally linked to a synagogue. |
| *Bentsh* (Y) | The custom of saying grace after a meal. |
| *B'vakasha* (H) | Please. Also used in sense of "you're welcome." |
| *Bikur Cholim* | Visiting the sick. An important Jewish practice; some synagogues rotate the privilege/*mitzvah* among their congregants. |
| *Birkat Hachodesh* | Blessing of the new month. |
| *B'rachah* (H) | A blessing. |
| *Bris* or *Brit* | Circumcision. |
| *Bubba* (Y) | Grandma. (*Bubba maises*—old wives' tales.) |
| *Chai* (H) | Life. In number, the equivalent of eighteen. |
| *Chalila* | Heaven forbid! |
| *Challah* | Braided Sabbath bread, also used for holidays. |

| | |
|---|---|
| *Chanukat Habayit* | A house warming festivity. Can be a private home or a public institution. |
| *Chazan* (H) | Cantor. |
| *Chazir* | Pig. Sometimes used pejoratively about a person. |
| *Cherem* | Excommunication. |
| *Chevra kadisha* | Burial society. |
| *Chochem* | A sage. Sometimes used to mean a "wise guy." |
| *Chuppah* (H) | Wedding canopy. |
| *Churban* | Destruction. Used in Yiddish to refer to Holocaust. |
| *Chutzpah* (H) | Unmitigated gall. |
| | |
| *Daven* | To pray. Some people link this word to "divine." |
| *Drei Kopp* (Y) | A manipulator; someone to be on guard against. |
| *Dreidel* (Y) | A top, used during Hanukkah games. Known in Hebrew as *s'vivon*. |
| *D'rosha* (Y) | A sermon, particularly in an Orthodox synagogue where the rabbi flavors his talk with Yiddish phrases. |
| | |
| *Emes* (Y) | Truth. Hebrew equivalent is *Emet*. |
| *Erev* | Eve (of) Sabbath, holidays, and fasts. |
| *Eretz Israel* | Land of Israel. |
| | |
| *Fleishig* (Y) | Foods that are classified under meat label as opposed to those listed as dairy foods. |
| | |
| *Gan Eden* | Garden of Eden; heaven. |
| *Gefilte fish* (Y) | Popular Jewish fish concoction served on Sabbath and holidays. |
| *Gematriah* | System whereby Hebrew letters all have |

|                      |                                                                                                                              |
|----------------------|------------------------------------------------------------------------------------------------------------------------------|
|                      | numerical values; some people read mystical values into interpretation.                                                       |
| *Genizah* (H)        | Hiding place, usually in synagogue, for discarded holy books and documents no longer usable.                                  |
| *Ger*                | A male convert to Judaism.                                                                                                     |
| *Gevalt* (Y)         | Help! Emergency!                                                                                                              |
| *G'lila* (H)         | Honor accorded to person called to Torah to "roll" the scroll together and tie it in preparation for its return to ark.       |
| *Golus* (Y)          | Exile, Diaspora. Hebrew equivalent is *galut*.                                                                                |
| *Goy*                | A Gentile.                                                                                                                     |
| *G'yoret* (H)        | A female convert to Judaism.                                                                                                   |
| *Hagba*              | Honor of being called to "raise" the Torah, before it is prepared for return to ark.                                          |
| *Haggadah*           | The Passover booklet that lays out the seder.                                                                                  |
| *Halachah* (H)       | Jewish religious law.                                                                                                         |
| *Hamantasch* (Y)     | Traditional three-cornered Purim pastry.                                                                                       |
| *Hatikvah*           | Israel's anthem. Literally "the hope."                                                                                        |
| *Havdalah* (H)       | Closing ceremony on Saturday evening, ushering Sabbath out until the next week. Synagogue service includes special candle-lighting, incense smelling. |
| *Hechsher*           | Permission, usually referring to *kashrut* supervision.                                                                       |
| *Heymish* (Y)        | Homelike, unpretentious.                                                                                                     |
| *Im Yirtze HaShem*   | God willing! (Sometimes mispronounced as *mirtze shem*.)                                                                      |

| | |
|---|---|
| *Kaballah* | Jewish mysticism. |
| *Kaftan* | Long coat worn by Hassidic Jews. |
| *Kain ain hara* (Y) | Exclamation comparable to, "the evil eye shall not befall" someone. |
| *Kallah* | A bride. |
| *Ketuba* | Marriage contract. |
| *Khazars* | A Turkish people who embraced Judaism in the eighth century. |
| *Kibbitz* (Y) | To horse around; to deflate someone's overblown ego. |
| *Kibbutz* | An Israeli agricultural collective settlement. |
| *Kiddush* | Sabbath and holiday eve blessing for wine. |
| *Kipah* (H) | Hebrew word for *yarmulke*. (Plural is *kipot*.) |
| *Kittel* | White overgarment worn by Orthodox groom at wedding ceremony; also used during High Holy Days. |
| *Kotel* (H) | The Western Wall in Jerusalem, now a major holy place. |
| *Kugel* (Y) | Pudding |
| *Landsman* (Y) | A person who came from the same town or area as you. |
| *L'Chayim!* | To life! A toast. |
| *Luach* (H) | A calendar, generally meant as the Jewish calendar. |
| *Maariv* | Evening service. |
| *Maot Chitim* | Pre-Passover charitable gifts (usually food, clothes) to needy people. |
| *Mashgiach* (H) | *Kashrut* supervisor. |
| *Mashiach* | Messiah. |
| *Mazel Tov* | Good luck. |

| | |
|---|---|
| *Melamed* | A religious teacher. Sometimes connotes a poor, untalented simpleton. |
| *Menorah* | Candelabrum. Special menorah for Hanukkah: *Hanukkiyah*. |
| *Mensch* | A solid, full-fledged, good person. |
| *Meshugga* | Crazy, screwy, offbeat. |
| *Mezuzah* | Container affixed to doorpost holding biblical verses used at home, synagogue, and Jewish institutions. Many traditionalists kiss it with their fingers on entering and leaving. |
| *Mikvah* (H) | Ritual bath used by brides and women at conclusion of menstrual period. |
| *Milchig* (Y) | Dairy foods. |
| *Minyan* | A quorum of ten adult males needed for religious service; some synagogues now include women in the count. |
| *Mishpachah* (H) | Family. |
| *Mitzvah* | Commandment; a good deed. |
| *Mohel* (H) | Specially trained man who performs circumcision. |
| *Neshama* | Soul. |
| *Nigun* (H, Y) | Melody sometimes used to describe wordless Hassidic tunes. |
| *Nusach* | A communal style of religious service. There are small differences between Ashkenazic and Sephardic rites. |
| *Olov HaShalom* (H) | May he rest in peace. (For a woman: *Ole-ha hashalom*.) |
| *Oneg Shabbat* | Literally, "Sabbath Delight." Festive Saturday afternoon gathering featuring study and singing. |

| | |
|---|---|
| *Pareve* | Neutral, referring to food that is neither dairy nor meat. |
| *Parochet* | Special curtain that hangs in front of Holy Ark in synagogue. |
| *Payes* (Y) | In Hebrew, *payot.* Sidecurls worn by some Orthodox men and boys. |
| *Pesach* | Hebrew for Passover (also used in Yiddish). Many wish one another a "zeese Pesach" (sweet Passover). |
| *Pikuach Nefesh* | Saving a life. Jewish law states that saving a life is more important than any religious commandment. |
| *Pushka* (Y) | Traditional charity box found in many Jewish homes. |
| *Reb* | An honorific title, used with man's first name, often attesting to person's character and/or knowledge. |
| *Rebbe* | Rabbi. Used primarily by Hassidic Jews. |
| *Refuah shlayma* (H) | Full recovery. A traditional wish for an ill person. |
| *Rosh Chodesh* | First day of new month, when additional prayers are added to service. |
| *Sabra* | Native-born Israeli. |
| *Sedra* | Weekly biblical portion read at Sabbath service. |
| *Sephardic* | Jews who came originally from Spain and Mediterranean basin countries. |
| *Shabbat Hagadol* | "The great Sabbath"—Sabbath before Passover. |
| *Shabbes goy* | "Sabbath Gentile." Referring to Gentiles who used to light fires on Sabbath for traditional families for pay. |

| | |
|---|---|
| *Shachrit* | Morning service. |
| *Shadchan* | Matchmaker. The match is known as a *shiduch*. |
| *Shaila* | A religious question posed to a rabbi. |
| *Shaitel* (Y) | A wig worn by Orthodox married women. |
| *Shechinah* | Divine presence. |
| *Shema Yisrael* | "Hear O Israel!" First words of main Jewish prayer. |
| *Shicker* (Y) | A drunkard. |
| *Shiksa* | Gentile young woman. |
| *Shlep* (Y) | To pull or tote. |
| *Shomer Shabbat* (H) | Sabbath observer. |
| *Shtetl* (Y) | Traditional Jewish hamlet of century ago. |
| *Shul* (Y) | Popular term for synagogue; literally "school" because study aspect of synagogue always took precedence. |
| *S'micha* (H) | Ordination (for a rabbi). |
| *Sofer* | A scribe for Torah scrolls, *tefillin*, and mezuzahs. |
| *Tallit* | Prayer shawl |
| *Tanach* (H) | Acronym for "Torah, N'Vi-im, K'tuvim" (entire Jewish Bible: Pentateuch, Prophets, Holy Writings). |
| *Tefillin* | Phylacteries, used by men at morning services (except on Sabbath and holidays). |
| *T'filat haderech* | A special prayer for a journey, asking God's guidance. |
| *Traif* (Y) | Not kosher. Refers to food; sometimes also used as a derogatory comment about a film, art, and so forth. |

| | |
|---|---|
| *Tsaddik* | A righteous person—the highest possible compliment. |
| *Ulpan* | An intensive course designed to teach Hebrew, used extensively for new immigrants in Israel. |
| *Vidui* | Confession. Special prayers on Yom Kippur are called confessionals. A dying person sometimes offers a vidui. |
| *Yahrzeit* (Y) | Annual commemoration of death of loved one, marked by recitation of *kaddish* and lighting of special lamp. |
| *Yenta* (Y) | A gossip; sometimes also a shrew. Used primarily to describe certain coarse women. |
| *Yeshiva* | A school for religious studies, mainly for students up to adulthood. Adults who study full-time enroll in a school called a *kolel*. |
| *Yichus* | Family pedigree, usually includes rabbinical/scholarly antecedents. |
| *Yizkor* | Memorial prayer included four times a year during Passover, Shavuot, Shmini Atzeret, and Yom Kippur. |
| *Zeyda* (Y) | Grandpa. |

# INDEX

Adon Olam, 82
Ahad Haam, 40
Ahavath Yisrael, 67
Aitz Chayim, 180
Akiva, Rabbi, 100
Alcoholics Anonymous, 35
Amidah, 96
art, 24
Ashkenazi, 63
aufruf, 9

Baal Koreh, 179
Baal Teshuva, 71
Baal Shem Tov, 7
Baal t'kiyah, 179
Babylonia, 51
Balfour Declaration, 163
Bay Psalm Book, 51
Ben-Gurion, David, 59
Benny, Jack, 83
bentshen, 39
Bialik, Chaim Nachman, 36
bimah, 106
Boro Park, 29
Brandeis, 27
breastplate, 179
bris, 121
Browne, Lewis, 49
Burton, Richard, 66
cantor, 179
challah, 38
chametz, 145
chatan, 106

Chevra kadisha, 128
chupah, 106
chutzpah, 89
Cincinnati, 65
Colorado, 57
Columbia, 51
Cyrus, 160

Dead Sea Scrolls, 164
Declaration of Independence, 56
divorce, 45
Dubnow, 70

Eban, Abba, 120
Ecclesiastes, 49
Einstein, 27
Encyclopedia Judaica, 82
ethical will, 60
Ethics of the Fathers, 41
Ethiopia, 80
etrog, 140

Fleg, Edmond, 25
Forward, 83
Frank, Leo, 172

gabbai, 78
Gamblers Anonymous, 35
get, 132
Ghandi, Mahatma, 20
Glilah, 111
Gorbachev, 90
Graetz, 70

greetings, 110
grogger, 144

haftorah, 39
hagbah, 111
Haggadah, 25
Halachah, 42
Halevi, Yehuda, 41
Hanukkiyah, 142
Harvard, 51
Hassidim, 64
havdalah, 39
Havurah, 51
Hatikvah, 114
Heine, 115
Hirsch, E. G., 71
Herzl, 65
Herzog, Haim, 16
Hillel, 63
Hoffer, Eric, 28
Holmes, Oliver Wendell, 149

Ibn-Ezra, 4
Iraq, 80
Israel Independence Day, 114

Jefferson, Thomas, 73
Johnson, Lyndon, 120
Joint Distribution Comm., 120

kaddish, 38
kalah, 106
Kaplan, Aryeh, 50
Karaites, 64
kashrut, 150
ketubah, 106
kibbutzim, 65
kiddush, 38
kipah, 91
kohen, 79
Kook, Isaac, 170
Krochmal, Nachman, 165

Ladino, 167
Las Vegas, 101
Lazare, Bernard, 72
Liberty Bell, 57
Living Torah, 50
Lowdermilk, Inez, 72
Lubavitch, 67
lulav, 140
Luzzato, 64

Maccabees, 161
machzor, 94
Magen David, 94
Maimonides, 60
Malachi, 57
maven, 89
mazel Tov, 107
Merchant of Venice, 46
Meshed, 163
Messiah, 65
Messina, 10
metziah, 89
mi sheh-bayrach, 94
Mitnagdim, 64
mitzvot, 53
mizrach, 180
Montefiore, 74
Mossad, 123
motzi, 92

Nachmanides, 7
Nasser, Gamal Abdel, 120
Ne'ila, 140
Ner Tamid, 180
Newman, Paul, 19

O'Brein, Cruise Connor, 30

Pesach, 144
Pidyon Ha-Ben, 124
pilgrims, 56

Pharisees, 63
Protocols of Elders of Zion, 16
pushka, 93

Queen Sabbath, 39

Rabbanites, 64
Rabbi, 179
Rashi, 79
Reagan, President, 90
Refuah Shlaymah, 94
reform, 65
Religon, Civil, 32
Renan, 72
Responsa, 24
Revelation, 7
Reykjavik, 17
rimonim, 179
Riskin, Shlomo, 67
Robinson, Edward G, 82
Rome, 71
Rosh Hashanah, 136
Roth, Cecil, 82

Sabbath, 41
Sadducees, 63
Salk, 57
sandak, 123
Schechter, Solomon, 27
Senate, 46
Sephardic, 63
Shalom Bayit, 132
Shalosh Seudot, 41
Shammai, 63
shammas, 89
Sharansky, Natan, 20
Shema, 91
shiva, 130
shloshim, 131
shmir, 89
shofar, 136
shomer, 129

shuckeling, 94
shul, 91
siddur, 94
Siege, The, 30
Silverman, Morris, 56
simcha, 101
sufganiyah, 142
sukkot, 56
Swope, Gerard, 4

Taiwan, 16
tallit, 48
Taylor, Elizabeth, 66
tefillin, 48
Thanksgiving, 56
tickets, Holiday, 104
tikkun Olam, 47
Todd, Mike, 66
Tolstoy, 69
Tsedaka, 9
Tsedek, 9
Twain, Mark, 27

United Jewish Appeal, 120

Warsaw Ghetto, 55
Waterloo, 48
Weizmann, 65
Why I Am A Jew, 25
Wise, Isaac Mayer, 65

Yahrzeit, 92
Yale, 51
Yasher Ko-ach, 110
Yemen, 80
Yeshiva, 179
Yeshiva University, 163
Yizkor, 54
Yom Kippur, 136

Zangwill, Israel, 114
z'mirot, 38